Also available from Worldwide Mystery by
ERIC WRIGHT

A FINE ITALIAN HAND
FINAL CUT
A SENSITIVE CASE
A QUESTION OF MURDER

ERIC WRIGHT

DEATH *by* DEGREES

WORLDWIDE.

TORONTO • NEW YORK • LONDON
AMSTERDAM • PARIS • SYDNEY • HAMBURG
STOCKHOLM • ATHENS • TOKYO • MILAN
MADRID • WARSAW • BUDAPEST • AUCKLAND

DEATH BY DEGREES

A Worldwide Mystery/June 1995

This edition is reprinted by arrangement with Scribner, an imprint of Simon & Schuster, Inc.

ISBN 0-373-26169-1

Printed in U.S.A.

FOR HOWARD ENGEL

PROLOGUE

BY MARCH the preliminary skirmishing was completed. The chair of the committee, feeling sure of enough votes to elect the administration's candidate, had proposed that the search for a Dean of Related Studies be confined to insiders. The faculty members of the committee, divided as they were on other issues, were united in not wanting the job to go to a stranger, and agreed immediately. The usual letters were sent to all the outsiders who had applied in response to the obligatory newspaper advertisement, thanking them for their interest.

In April the committee interviewed the four insiders, one a week on Wednesday afternoons, until there was nothing left to do but vote. By the first of May the choice lay between two, Jennifer Benson or Maurice Lyall. Lyall was the administration's man; Jennifer Benson was the candidate of the politically active members of the faculty. The other two had no chance at all.

The chairman of the committee, Joan Dooley, Vice-President of Human Affairs, began to worry that she had counted wrong, and pleaded for more time. 'I mean, hell's bells,' she said, 'you guys [by which she meant also Shirley Marconi] have worked real hard on this, and I'd like us to make a decision that we can all feel good about. Let's take another half-hour and go round the table, share our views once more. OK?

Gerald?' She turned to a neat little fair-haired man in his fifties who was indicating that he wished to speak.

'I have nothing more to say, today, tomorrow or any other day,' Gerald Pentes said. 'The discussion is meaningless because some people present have no intention of being informed by the rest of us. So let's get on with it.' He closed the folder in front of him and pushed it rudely at the chairman.

A current of irritation ran around the table. Pentes was famous among his colleagues for his temper tantrums, usually thrown because of his objection to some harmless bit of accommodation, like giving a student half a mark to allow him to graduate, but seen by Pentes as a major corruption of standards. He ought not to have been on a committee that was bound to have to compromise even to agree on procedures, but the president had persuaded him to sit as one of the administration's appointees, judging that Pentes would be so flattered by the president's attention that he would be certain to vote for the administration's candidate. But Pentes, as well as being proud of his integrity, was also silly enough to believe that he had caught the eye of the president for just that quality.

Fred Leitch, the new assistant registrar, looked at the ceiling and sucked his teeth.

Wilf Schreiber, faculty representative said, 'The whole point of the committee is to allow us to persuade each other, Gerald.'

'This thing has been rigged from the start,' Pentes said.

'I kind of resent that, Gerald,' the chairman of the committee said, but without anger, more in pain, rather. 'I wish I knew *how* to rig it. We could all be at home by now.' She chuckled, and shook her head with a rueful air.

'Sheer hypocrisy,' Pentes said, and this time he stung her. While she served an administration that had acquired its share of tarnish, she depended for her self-regard on being seen, or at least treated, as the honest broker between a president who was a creature of the board, and a faculty dominated (in the view of the board) by a trade union approach to its interests. 'I still want to hear everybody one more time,' she said, stiffly, pushing Pentes' folder back at him. 'Fred, start us off.'

And so the ritual resumed. Each member of the committee spoke about the good and bad points of each candidate, taking pride in concealing whom they favoured, for the ballot was secret. All except Fred Leitch, who spoke first. This was Leitch's first job in academe. He was freshly arrived from the fund-raising office of the party in power which was almost certainly going to lose the next election, and jobs had had to be found for the non-elected politicians until the party returned to office. Leitch wasn't sufficiently senior to be made a senator, for which there was a lot of competition, anyway, or even be offered a job on the Harbour Commission, and so Bathurst College had acquired an assistant registrar. Now he said, 'Lyall's the guy with experience, but Benson is the one with the brains, I guess, though she'd tear the place apart in a month. The other two are nowhere.' He looked at his watch. 'Couldn't organize a...' He paused, searching for a polite ending. 'A wienie roast,' he concluded.

'Wilf?' The chairman asked Schreiber to speak.

Schreiber spoke for about fifteen minutes about his experience with the main candidates, said how objectionable he found Leitch's description of the fringe candidates, his colleagues, and gave no clue as to how he would vote, although no one around the table had any doubt.

'Shirley?'

Shirley Marconi was the only unknown factor in the room. She had been elected by the faculty, because, although entirely unconnected with the faculty union, under the system of voting—a variety of proportional representation—she was the first choice of a minority of the faculty who voted against faculty politicians like Schreiber. 'I must urge the claims of a woman, I suppose, but I wonder if Jennifer Benson isn't too... controversial,' she said, leaving a clear impression that she would vote for Lyall.

Erroll Czerny-Smith, the French teacher, was next. After a five-minute discussion of the strong points of Maurice Lyall, whom he was widely known to detest, he ended by saying he had been very impressed by Benson in the interview.

'Your turn, Gerald,' Joan Dooley said reluctantly, for Pentes had not even turned his head as each member spoke, inviting everyone to notice his continuing hostility.

He looked out the window at the traffic on Bathurst Street. 'I have nothing to say,' he said, like a sulking ten-year-old.

It was on everyone's mind, then, that Maurice Lyall had the votes of Fred Leitch and Shirley Marconi, and that Jennifer Benson was supported by Wilf Schreiber and Czerny-Smith, just as everyone had expected.

But it was impossible to guess what Gerald Pentes would do in his emotionally charged state. Until now he was understood to be in the administration's camp, thus giving the nod to Lyall, but something had clearly upset him.

Joan Dooley lifted herself off her chair and pulled her khaki dress straight under her legs. She looked quickly around the table and winked. 'Let's adjourn until Wednesday at four. We'll have one more quick chat, and vote.' She said this as if she was proposing something slightly daring, like adjourning to a pub.

BUT BY WEDNESDAY a curious, and, for the administration, alarming shift had occurred. Gerald Pentes was still steaming, silent, immovable, and none of the others wanted to say anything more. But when they voted, there were now three for Jennifer Benson, the faculty's choice, one for Lyall, and there was one abstention.

Wilf Schreiber looked amazed, and Czerny-Smith reacted with the quiet pleasure of one who has completed a particularly difficult crossword puzzle. Shirley Marconi nearly succeeded in looking blank, but her pleasure showed, and Gerald Pentes was sufficiently jolted out of his injured stance to cast a look of vindictive satisfaction at Fred Leitch, who looked at the ceiling.

Under the rules, the president of the college could refuse to accept the committee's recommendation, and the board of governors could exercise its veto even if he accepted it, but such power was not invoked lightly and it looked as if they would have to take Jennifer Benson, a notorious demonstrator and organizer of protests both on and off the campus, as the new Dean of Related Studies.

'Waal,' the chairman began, in her 'just-plain-folks' manner. 'Looks like we've got a pretty clear recommendation.' She seemed to want to avoid speaking the name of the winner until she had to. 'Any comments?' she asked.

Czerny-Smith, Schreiber and Marconi shook their heads, wanting to hear the magic words said. Gerald Pentes sat mute. Fred Leitch said, 'It's not a valid vote, of course.'

Marconi said, 'That's ridiculous.' Czerny-Smith muttered 'Obstructionism. Let's get on.' Schreiber, after several seconds, said, 'As the original author of the report that governs these proceedings, I can vouch that the vote *is* legal.'

Fred Leitch said, 'You wrote the original, but you didn't read the latest version, I guess.'

'What's that supposed to mean?' Schreiber snapped, jolted out of his regular stance of amused pundit.

'The rules say "no abstentions".'

'What rules?' Marconi wanted to know.

'Nothing of the kind,' Schreiber said.

Shirley Marconi said, 'We had an abstention on the last committee I was on.'

Joan Dooley leaned towards Leitch. 'What does it say, Fred?'

In the babble, Gerald Pentes' cry of 'But you told me I *could* abstain,' was lost.

In the following silence, Leitch said, first to Pentes, 'Sorry, Gerald, I was wrong.' Then to Schreiber, 'Amendment No. 17 was introduced because of a deadlock, they tell me. After your time I guess, eh, Wilf?'

The chairman thumbed excitedly through a thick document, found what she was looking for, read it, and held it up. 'I'm afraid Fred's right. Now what?'

'We'll have to vote again,' Leitch said. 'But not tonight. We agreed, come what may, to cut it off at six. It's six-fifteen and tonight's my anniversary.' He got up and left.

'Now what?' Schreiber inquired. 'No doubt we'll hear from Mr Leitch what our next move is.'

'Can we take five? Shirley Marconi asked. 'I need a pee.' Not waiting for an answer, she headed for the door, her cigarettes already in her hand.

When she returned, Joan Dooley said, 'We'll go at it one more time. Friday at four, please, and no excuses, you guys, eh? And would whoever abstained please come to a decision.' She smiled and shook her head to show she was not giving orders, just asking people to play the game.

'It could have been Leitch himself,' Schreiber pointed out, recovering.

'That would have been pretty irresponsible, knowing what he did,' Dooley protested.

'Or clever.'

AND SO THEY MET on Friday and the chairman went rapidly round the table for any last comments. Only Erroll Czerny-Smith had anything to add. He said he had been consulting what he called his constituents, and learned some things which had made him very glad that they had not proceeded in a hurry.

Joan Dooley called for the vote. The result this time was two for Jennifer Benson, two for Lyall and one for David Prince, one of the rank outsiders.

'What now, Wilf?' she asked Schreiber. After they had got over their shock, they all knew the answer, but they waited for Schreiber, the expert on procedure, to pronounce. 'I am obliged to say that the chairman has the casting vote,' he said finally.

'But, heck,' Dooley said, slapping both hands on the table in mock dismay, 'they're both such top-notch people, they all are. I hate to vote against any of them.'

'Then vote *for* one of them, so we can get the hell out of here,' Leitch said, apparently to himself. 'I've got a ball-game to go to.'

Hustled into it, Dooley said, 'Waal, OK. If I have to indicate a preference, then I guess I would have to say "Maurice".'

As soon as the name was out, Fred Leitch said, 'Lyall it is. You need us any more?' He stood up to show he was speaking rhetorically, nodded all round, winked at Gerald Pentes and left.

Pentes, Joan Dooley and Czerny-Smith quickly followed him out. None of them looked at each other.

Left in the room with Schreiber, Shirley Marconi said, 'Bastard!'

Schreiber said, 'It's all in the game, Shirley. Politics is his trade. You see how clever that was? Before the last meeting he persuaded Gerald to abstain. If we had then voted for Maurice Lyall that would have been that, you wouldn't have heard anything more about illegal abstentions, or not until too late. But when we plumped for Benson, Leitch had a rabbit to pull out of his hat. I must remember that one.'

Marconi said, 'I wasn't talking about him. I was talking about Maurice fucking Lyall.'

'That makes it clear where your vote went. So did mine.'

'Then who voted for Lyall, apart from Leitch?'

'Whoever switched from Jennifer. Not Gerald Pentes, I think. I suppose that's what Erroll meant when he said he had been listening to his constituents. He was warning us he was about to switch. He ran away afterwards so he wouldn't have to talk about it. Who knows why? But what about you, Shirley? You're very *anti*-Lyall all of a sudden. Why the switch? Your constituents put you here to restore the balance upset by left-wingers like Erroll and me. Aren't they going to be annoyed with you?'

'They'll know why by the time they hear about the vote.' She walked to the door, holding another cigarette ready to be lit. 'Can't we protest?' she asked, exhaling the first lungful.

He raised his hands. 'It's all legal. I'm afraid now we've got the Vicar of Bray as dean. All we can do is make his life a misery.'

BUT TWO WEEKS LATER Maurice Lyall's life was over. He was found dead, shot in his own house on the night of Victoria Day.

ONE

STAFF INSPECTOR Charlie Salter pushed his chair back from his desk and tried to think of a distraction, something that would blot out the misery that was making it impossible for him to concentrate on what he was supposed to be writing.

A game of squash might do it, but that would mean going down to the club in the hope of picking up a partner. At nine-thirty in the morning, the chances were remote. He considered going for a walk, but the streets around the Toronto police headquarters offered no inducement for walking; they were so familiar they would just focus his mind. Maybe a walk to City Hall to talk to his first wife? His second wife, Annie, was doing more than her share already, but he hadn't talked to Gerry for a year, although they were still on good terms. She was a social worker of some kind; she would let him talk. Yes, he thought, that's the trick—talk about it instead of trying not to think about it. But he couldn't just walk in on her.

He picked up his phone and called the mayor's office and learned that the newly-elected mayor had her own staff and Gerry was gone, no one knew where, but if he wanted to leave his number they would pass it on if she called.

All he could think of now was the World's Biggest Bookstore, a few blocks south. Surely that was good for an hour? He picked his raincoat off the peg, still damp from the rain he had walked through on his way back from the hospital that morning, and left a message with the desk that he would be back by eleven.

WHEN THE CALL CAME on Sunday evening, his wife, Annie, had driven him immediately to the hospital where he found May, his father's common-law wife, sitting in the corridor outside the emergency ward. She did not even respond to his greeting, simply gesturing towards the door with both hands clenched tightly together.

Behind the door he found himself in a glass-walled room packed with machinery. Two or three nylon curtains divided the space into bed-sized pieces, in one of which he found his father attached with tubes and wires and oxygen mask to all the survival machines of the age. Salter wanted to unplug the lot immediately—he had always said he would—but he had not thought it through or imagined the circumstances accurately enough. It was already out of his hands. A nurse who had been watching a monitor turned round on her stool.

'You related?'

'I'm his son.'

She nodded at the line being recorded on the monitor. 'He's got a strong pulse.'

'How is he?'

'He's responding.' She put a metal chair beside the bed. 'Here.'

He sat and looked at the bruised, sunken face for a few minutes, not knowing what to do, then remembered May. 'I'll be outside,' he said to the nurse.

In the corridor he took the seat next to May and tried to get the first gesture right. He had no sort of emotional bond with her, but in some sense she was his stepmother. She had been the widow of an old work-mate of his father's and she had made his father happy for the past ten years after a decade of glum loneliness as a widower. But in all the times she had visited Salter with his father, she never overcame her shyness enough to be able to manage more than a sentence or two of conversation. With him, anyway.

Now he reached towards her and she grabbed his hand and began kneading it fiercely.

'What happened?' he asked.

'Fell down the steps. Cut his head. The neighbours found him and sent for the ambulance right away. I was out visiting my sister.' She spoke even more quietly than usual, in a tiny, frightened voice.

'What did the doctor tell you?'

'No one's come out yet.'

Annie appeared and sat down on the other side of May. Salter told her all he had learned while she was parking the car. Annie put her arm around May's shoulders and Salter watched some of the tension ebb as May yielded to the comfort. 'Go and get some tea,' Annie ordered. 'Not from the machines in the basement. There's a take-out place still open across the street.'

Grateful for some instructions, Salter went off to find the store, trying not to think about the probability that his father was dying. When he returned, Annie had found the private room usually reserved for the doctors to communicate bad news. 'I got the key off a nurse,' Annie said.

Salter distributed the tea, and picked up a signal from Annie that he should leave. In the next half-hour he toured the corridors, returning every few minutes to see if he was wanted, while Annie heard a steadily more coherent May tell all the details of the crisis. Eventually he found an old *Time* magazine and settled on the bench outside their door.

There was one other patient waiting, a man in his early twenties with his arm in a sling. Salter guessed he had been in a fight. By his boots, his filthy jeans, his five-inch-wide leather belt and his sweatshirt imprinted with flames, he looked like someone who got into fights. Without any exchange of courtesies, the man said, 'I've bin arrested for smoking. Guess you can't smoke any more, eh?'

Salter, grateful enough for a distraction, wanted to point out that there was a warning on every pack, but this character lived too close to the edge for jokes, and they were alone in the corridor, so he just made a gesture, inviting more.

'Yeah,' the man said, inconsequentially.

'What happened to your arm?' Salter asked, to keep him going.

'They think it's broke. It just started hurting tonight. I did it two days ago.'

'Did what?'

'Rolled over.'

'In a car?'

'In my truck. I hit the ditch coming off the Markham turn-off. That's what they charged me for.'

'What did they charge you with?'

'Dangerous driving. Fucking accident, for Chrissake. I spent the night in the hospital. They thought I was concussed, because I said I couldn't remember how it happened. You know what they did? Shone a fucking flashlight in my eyes every hour and made me tell them my name. Every hour, all fucking night. They had this cop waiting until I remembered, see. I got pissed off with the fucking flashlight and told them what happened.'

'What did you say to them?'

'I told 'em, I was trying to light a fucking cigarette.'

'And you hit the ditch.'

'Yeah.'

'And they called that dangerous driving?'

'First they didn't. Then they asked me how I was trying to light it.'

'What did you say?'

'I had to use both hands, see. The lighter in the truck don't work, and the window's broke on my side, so you have to use both hands to keep the match going, see. So I had the wheel tucked between my knees. Then I hit a little bump and my knee slipped, and over I went.'

'You left the highway driving with your knees? And you told them that?'

'Yeah. They were testing my blood for drugs or booze and stuff. They coulda found somethin' from the day before. But I wasn't high. It was an accident.'

Salter could think of nothing to say. The man returned to his starting point. 'You ain't supposed to smoke when you're driving?' Then he pulled a cigarette from his pocket and searched for matches. Salter pointed to the NO SMOKING signs. 'Ah, shit,' the man said, and kicked his way through the EXIT door. He never returned.

That was the only diversion of the night. From time to time a patient was wheeled by en route to the elevator, but gradually the corridor grew quiet as the flow of accidents dried up, and then he was alone in the corridor. At midnight the nurse he had spoken to when he arrived walked by and Salter asked her if anything was happening that he could know about.

'He's going to get a CAT scan,' she said.

Salter put his head in the door of the waiting-room. 'He's going to get a CAT scan,' he said. 'What's that?'

'It's a routine check,' Annie said. 'My father had one when he bumped his head.' She frowned at Salter to shut up and go away. Salter checked the glass-walled room every fifteen minutes until two o'clock, when an orderly took pity on them and made some more tea. Still his father had not returned from the X-ray department. Whenever he looked in on Annie and May they seemed to be talking about May's girlhood in the Beaches.

At three o'clock in the morning a courteous East Indian doctor appeared and told them that there was no change, that his father's signs were stable, but that he would be staying in intensive care.

Salter now was ready to ask if his father might die, but not in front of the others, so he followed the doctor until they were out of earshot, and asked him as he was getting on to the elevator.

'How old is he?' the doctor asked in turn.

'Seventy-five or six.'

'Not old, then. He seems very strong. We'll know better tomorrow.'

'Today, you mean. Who will let me know?'

'We will.'

'I meant if you all forget. See, doctor, we've been sitting on that bench for the last five hours but no one said a word until you came along.'

'It has been a busy night.' The elevator came and the doctor reached out to hold the door open.

'No, it hasn't. I've been sitting here watching. One dead on arrival, one heart attack, a guy who left, and a bum who'd been in a fight. That's it.' Salter had rehearsed this speech in his head several times.

'The derelict was drunk and concussed. We shall have to watch him all night. And there was a considerable carryover from those admitted during the evening.'

'Somebody could've said something, though, couldn't they, after they passed us for the fiftieth time? Even the guy who mops floors felt sorry for us and made us a cup of tea.' Salter got hold of himself. 'I'm sorry, I'm talking to the wrong man. After all, you did stop, didn't you.'

The doctor's skin seemed to have three layers of colour: the top layer was the grey of fatigue; next came the natural brown skin of his sub-continent; beneath that there seemed to be another layer of grey, the edges of which were just visible around the eyes. 'The pictures we took show a slight fracture of the skull, and possibly a stroke. I want the specialist to have a look at them in the morning, but I do think he may have had a stroke which caused the fall. It's a common sequence. We'll know better tomorrow.'

'Will he die?' Salter asked again. He did not ask in anguish or fear, but in order to speak the words, to face the reality, and get used to it.

The doctor stepped back away from the elevator door. He looked at Salter appraisingly. 'He might,' he said. 'He might recover completely. And he might be permanently changed. I do not think he will die, but it is a possibility you must be aware of. I will know more later in the day when I have consulted. You should take those ladies home now. Come back in the morning if you like. You can telephone at any time to see how he is. Good night.' He stepped around Salter and into the elevator.

Salter returned to the waiting-room and gave them a slightly edited version of what he had just heard. 'Go home now, you two. I'll stay here.'

May shook her head. 'I can have a rest in there.' She pointed to a tiny room with a stretcher and a mattress. 'I don't want to go home. He could need me at any time.'

'*I'll* use the bed,' Salter said. '*You* go home and get some proper sleep. I'll see you in the morning.'

With that, May allowed Annie to lead her away, and Salter lay down on the stretcher. But sleep was impossible, and at six he went to check on his father and found him awake and writhing in misery. He gave no sign that he recognized Salter. A doctor was examining him by looking at a monitor on the wall. In a corner, two nurses were talking about their leave schedules. As Salter looked around, waiting for someone to do something about his father's discomfort, or even ask Salter who he was, another nurse appeared and conferred with the doctor for a minute.

As she was leaving she glanced at the bed and frowned. 'That patient is very frightened,' she said to the doctor. 'He needs a sedative.'

The doctor glanced at the old man, nodded and said something to one of the nurses, who opened a cabinet and added something to the liquid into his arm. In a very few minutes his body sagged slightly and he fell asleep.

Salter followed the nurse into the hall and asked for a moment of her time. She waited, glancing at her watch.

'I'm his son. How is he?'

'He's pretty stable.'

'What does that mean? Will he live? Will he die? Will he be paralysed, crippled, able to talk? I'd like to know. And how long has he been lying there with three people in the room waiting for you to come along and notice he was in agony.'

'Steady,' she said. She took his arm and walked him to a quiet part of the corridor. 'I'm just a nurse,' she said. 'But I can confirm that your father has a slight fracture of the skull, and the scan showed that he probably had a few minor strokes in the past little while, and perhaps a major one before he fell. But his heart is fine, and so is his blood pressure. We are giving him antibiotics to avoid pneumonia, and some pain-reliever, as well as fluids. Yes, and a sedative. We've taken him off the oxygen, though. Anything else?'

'Yes. Why doesn't someone have the job of asking people who are sitting in the corridor all night if there's anything they'd like to know? Every couple of hours, say. I know it's the emergency ward, but you people act like it's you that are having the emergency, not the patients. You know, like it's wartime or something.'

'You've got a point. Why don't you take it up with someone? Not me. What they need is an ombudsperson—a patients' relatives' representative.'

'Right. Hire some old doctors. Someone who knows the language with the right to find out for the rest of us what the hell is happening.'

'Easy, boy. Tell them, if you can find out who "they" are. In the meantime, I'm the senior on duty and until twelve tonight you can ask me.'

'All right. And thanks for whatever you did back there.'

At eight o'clock Annie and May arrived and Salter made the best he could of what little news he had for May. Then he realized that the women had arrived together. 'Did you pick her up?' he asked Annie when May was in with his father.

'She's staying with us for the duration. She wants to do the day shift now, so we can leave her for the morning at least. I'll take you home. You need some sleep. I didn't get much, but more than you, I bet.'

'I'll take a last look. Want to come in?'

Annie shook her head, and Salter joined May beside his father's bed.

He was lying quietly, staring at the ceiling. When Salter touched his hand he turned his head, looked at Salter, and tried to moisten his lips with his tongue. 'Soon be Christmas,' he whispered. 'You be a good boy.'

'It's only June, Dad,' Salter said, responding to an instinct to restore his father to the real world from wherever he was. Then he checked himself as he wondered if it might not be better to go along with his father's dream state, to accept it temporarily, and try to inhabit it. It was a problem that would recur frequently in the days ahead.

'He's hallucinating,' a nurse who was fiddling at a nearby sink said. 'It's the drug he's on.'

'At least he's peaceful.'

'He is,' the nurse agreed. 'Not all of them are.'

When Salter and Annie returned to the hospital after lunch his father was still in intensive care, and May was still sitting in the corridor. No one had spoken to her so far. Annie took her out of the building for a walk, while Salter went in to see his father.

It seemed to Salter that either he was getting used to him or that his father looked significantly better than he had that morning, and he was sleeping calmly. Salter asked one of the nurses to tell him which doctor was in charge now, but as she was about to respond the East Indian doctor reappeared.

Salter said, 'Are you still on duty?'

'Twenty-four hours. I finish this afternoon. Now, your father is very stable at the moment, and I am going to move him to a medical ward. We want to keep him under observation for a while. Will he be going back to a good situation?'

'What's that?'

'Is he in a retirement home, or a nursing home where he can get proper care?'

'He lives at home. I suppose he'll have to go into a nursing home now. His wife won't be able to manage. Has he had a stroke, by the way?'

'Yes, he has. Dr Chares confirmed it. But he could recover to ninety-five per cent of his old self.'

'Would you talk to his wife, doctor.'

He looked at his watch. 'I am off duty now.'

'Here they are. Two minutes,' Salter pleaded.

Salter walked along the corridor to meet them and reported the substance of his conversation, while the doctor waited.

'I'm taking him home,' May said.

Annie looked away. Salter said, 'He could be too much for you, May.'

'I'm taking him home.'

They waited for the doctor to dissuade her.

'Before you start,' May said, when the doctor joined them, 'I'm taking him home.' It was a whole new May, tough and probably immovable.

'We would need to be sure you could manage before we discharged him.'

'Then you'll have to keep him until you're sure, won't you? When he's well enough for you to discharge, then he'll be well enough for me to take home.'

'Good,' the doctor said. 'Because that's where he belongs, if possible. Just find out about the support services that are available to help you to look after him until he's back on his feet.' He addressed himself to Salter.

'At home,' May reminded him.

Annie interjected. 'I gather you people are in favour of home care wherever possible,' she said, slowly and loudly.

The doctor nodded gratefully, realizing that Annie was speaking to drive the point home to May. 'Some of us are, very much. In our experience people who stay at home tend to live longer, and stay happier. Eventually the time comes, especially if they live alone, when they can no longer manage, but until then . . .'

'He's not alone,' May said. 'I'm looking after him.' But Annie's interjection had allowed enough time for her to realize that they were not about to carry her husband off to a nursing home.

'When he is a little better, you must ask to see the social worker, who can explain everything to you,' the doctor said. 'And now, please, I have to go.'

May stayed in the hospital to watch over the move, Annie arranged to return later in the day, and Salter walked over to his office to try to do a little work.

TWO

As HEAD and usually sole member of the Special Affairs Unit, Salter reported directly to the deputy chief, handling whatever crossed the deputy's desk that did not fit the work descriptions of the regular units, or, for one reason or another, needed particular attention. At the moment, having recently come off a case that involved finding out something about Toronto's gambling fraternity, he had been trying to assemble the arguments for and against off-track betting and casinos. Both were illegal in Ontario, but the government had done so well out of lotteries in recent years that it was now proposing cutting down the provincial debt with a rake-off from legalized gambling, in the teeth of the opposition of the more evangelical portion of the electorate, a group that traditionally contained a very high percentage of people who actually voted. Many Torontonians still liked the idea of keeping Toronto pure—one neighbourhood was still dry—and driving across the border to Buffalo for sin. But now most of the old forbidden pleasures like Sunday drinking and hard core pornography were available even in St Catharines, Ontario. There was hardly an illicit thrill left except smuggling cheap groceries across the International Peace Bridge on Sundays.

And gambling. The party in power owned some of its existence to the Nonconformist church, particularly to a Baptist minister, a spell-binding preacher and

crusader for social reform in the decades before pros-
perity. The problem for the remnants of this wing of
the party was whether gambling, like drink, rotted the
social fabric; the problem for the professional politicians in the cabinet was whether there was enough
money in it to make it worth offending the Baptists.
The question that the deputy had handed Salter was,
what were the implications for police work of imple-
menting any of the forms of gambling being proposed? At this stage Salter was spending most of his
day reading material supplied by a friend of his wife's,
a librarian in the centre for criminological studies at
the university. Now, though, the language of sociol-
ogy could not distract him from his private misery, and
thus he had decided to wander off to the World's Biggest Bookstore in search of distraction.

On his way out he paused in the open doorway of
Inspector Marinelli of the Homicide squad, hoping for
a chat. Marinelli looked up and waved him in. 'Read
this,' he said, as soon as Salter sat down. He handed
a sheet of paper across the desk.

*'Why have you not looked within for the hand that
struck Maurice Lyall down?'* read the message.

Marinelli handed over a second sheet. This one
read, *'If you are looking for an enemy of Maurice
Lyall, you have a wide choice in the groves of academe.'*

Salter took a third message from the homicide detective. It read, *'Why the cover-up? The establishment closing ranks?'*

'They all came in the last ten days, one after the
other,' Marinelli said.

'Who's Lyall?'

'A teacher at Bathurst Community College. He was shot on May 24 by someone who was robbing his house and got disturbed. There's no reason to suspect anyone around the college, or there wasn't, until these started to come in.'

Salter threw the messages on the desk. 'A crank,' he said. 'An educated one.'

'He's sending them to the papers, too. They've just turned them over to us, but they're interested. Until we find the killer, we have to worry about them doing a little story about these messages.'

Salter picked up the sheets of paper again and read the messages aloud. 'They don't sound too real, do they? Kind of fancy-wancy. Probably a shit-disturber. An academic shit-disturber who's been reading too much Sherlock Holmes. You've had them tested?'

'Sure. There are no prints. The paper is standard, sold by a stationery chain, and the thing was done on a word-processor.'

Salter wondered if this might be what he was looking for. 'Maybe you should investigate them.'

'How? Investigate what?'

'Send someone on to the campus, show them you're around.' Salter put some enthusiasm into his voice as an agenda appeared for him. 'Interview all Lyall's enemies and all his friends, too. That'll shut the writer up while you're looking for the guy who did it.'

Marinelli shook his head. 'My super's down with the 'flu, did you know? I'm in charge. I've got no time for crap like this. Fucking wild goose chase.'

Salter understood what Marinelli was saying. If by chance there was something real behind the note, it would not be a matter of questioning suspects. You would have to find out if there was anything in the internal workings or politics, especially the politics, of the college that would justify asking the hard questions. You couldn't just line up five hundred people and ask them where they were on the night of the twenty-fourth and to provide you with an example of their prose style, or maybe you could, but you should try and cut down the numbers by concentrating on the most likely, and to do that you had to find out what had been happening on the campus lately that Lyall was concerned with. It could take weeks. Just what he needed.

'I have,' he said.

Marinelli looked at him, waiting for an explanation.

'I'm trying to write a report on gambling, but I'm having a lot of trouble concentrating, so I'd like something to keep me busy for a while.'

'Until?'

'Until I find out if my father is going to make it. Yesterday I thought he was dying. Now it looks as if he might make it, but I'm spending a lot of time at the hospital, and bothering people like you.' Salter looked steadily at Marinelli to show he meant what he was saying.

Marinelli was embarrassed. After a respectful moment, he said, 'Yeah, someone said you had a problem at home. Were you—sorry—*are* you close?'

'We weren't last week. We are now.'

After another pause Marinelli said, 'I don't know how to fix it, Charlie. I can ask for extra help—we're swamped as usual—but I can't ask for you. Christ, you out-rank me.'

Salter gave a 'forget-it-then' shrug. Then he changed his mind and leaned towards Marinelli. 'You mind if I do? I'll go see the deputy now and tell him I'm useless. I can't keep my mind on the report; it might be better if I did something else for a while. I'll tell him I've been hearing from you about this anonymous letter-writer. I'll ask him if I can help out.'

'I don't know, Charlie. It makes me look kind of wimpy, doesn't it?'

'I don't want to take any leave. I'll go nuts.'

Marinelli looked away.

Salter pleaded, 'Phone him when I leave here, before I get to his office. Tell him I'm on my way, warn him that it's not your idea. He might buy it.'

'I'm telling you, Charlie, this guy was killed by some thug who got interrupted robbing his house. We'll find him soon.'

'I won't be looking for *him*. I'll look for the guy who's been writing these notes. Be interesting. Nothing to do with the real investigation. I'll leave you to do your job.'

'Or woman.'

'What? Right. Person. Phone Mackenzie, then phone me that you've done it before I go see him.' Salter tried to hustle Marinelli into action. He looked at his watch. 'I'll wait in my office.'

'OK. I *will* tell him it was your idea, though.'

TEN MINUTES LATER Salter got the call. Marinelli said, 'All set. He asked me what I thought, if I minded. He thinks it's a good idea, for you.'

So Marinelli had talked to Mackenzie about the need to find some therapeutic activity for him. That was all right. 'I'll come and get the story before I go off to the college.'

'WE GOT A CALL on Tuesday morning at ten-fifteen. A cleaning lady, Maria Madrid, let herself into a house on Gibson. That's the little street off Yonge opposite the Rosedale subway station. Backs on to the park. She found the place trashed. Maurice Lyall, the owner, was dead in the bedroom, shot with his own gun from about four feet away. At the moment we figure that someone broke in, Lyall heard them, tried to take them on and they got the better of him. The gun was clean except for one print of Lyall's which was smudged. We think the killer had gloves on.'

'He live alone?'

'Separated from his wife a while ago, about ten years. The cleaning lady says he had a girlfriend. This cleaning lady never saw her but sometimes she could tell there had been someone. Lipstick in the bathroom, something like that.'

'Monday was a holiday, a long weekend. Didn't he spend it with her?'

'You could find out. It was Victoria Day, remember.'

'Queen Victoria's Birthday.'

'What?'

'That's what it used to be called.'

'Yeah? Anyway, it's a big night for fireworks and all. He went to a street fireworks party on Victoria Day. It's illegal, but they still do it on some streets. He left the party when the actual fireworks started, around eight.'

'What time did he get killed?'

'Between eight and twelve.'

'Nobody saw anyone or heard the gun?'

'Fireworks, Charlie. The ideal night to let off a gun.'

'Then what?'

'Whoever did it just walked in—there was no sign of a break-in, but that doesn't mean much because Lyall didn't use to lock his doors. The place had been trashed from top to bottom. We still aren't sure what they got. Piece of antique silver, his watch, the cleaning lady said, but we don't know what else.'

'Stereo? TV?'

'None of those. That's why we figure it was someone looking for a quick hit, stuff he could put in his pockets.'

'Then he got interrupted by Lyall?'

'That's what we think. We figure Lyall was reading in the bedroom and he heard the guy and tried to stop him.'

'Where did he keep the gun?'

'In the basement.' Marinelli leaned back, waiting for Salter to see the obvious. Then, to save trouble, he said, 'I don't know, maybe that night he took it to bed with him. Kinky.'

'If he didn't, you're saying he heard someone moving around, went down two flights of stairs to the basement, went back up to his bedroom, all without being seen by the guy, waited in his bedroom for him, but then when the guy came to him he somehow got the gun off Lyall and blew him away?'

'We don't know. Maybe Lyall tried to jump him. And there could have been two of them. We don't know.'

'What's the address on Gibson?'

Marinelli opened a desk drawer. 'You want to take a look? Here.' He threw a key with the label attached across the desk. 'It's been tidied up. Here's some pictures of the way we found it.'

Salter flipped through them. Every room in the house had been turned over. The drawers in the kitchen and bedrooms had been emptied on to the floor, and books in the study pulled from the shelves. It might be enough, he thought, to keep his mind off his father. 'I'll poke around. Bathurst College is downtown, right?'

'South of Dundas, off Bathurst Street. Enjoy yourself. Sorry about your dad.'

THE HOUSES on the south side of Gibson Avenue back on to a wide lane and a row of parking spaces. Beyond the lane, a municipal park serves the neighbourhood with a children's playground and some tennis courts. Once Gibson Avenue was a working-class street, a jumble of small houses crammed into tiny lots, but the park and the subway have long since raised the value of the real estate in the area to a level beyond the reach of any artisan.

Salter walked down the side of Lyall's house and into the back yard where a small patch of lawn ended at a giant maple and a fence with a space for a gate. Anyone leaving the house in a hurry could disappear along the lane and from there into the park.

He crossed the stone patio and tried the back door, but it was now locked. He let himself in through the main door, wondering why it was on the side of the house, then saw that the house had been gutted to make new living space. The entire front of the house, to the left of the small hall, was taken up with the kitchen. The back was now one large room which led to the garden doors. On the second floor there were two bedrooms, a bathroom, and a study. Salter established which was Lyall's bedroom, then continued up to the third floor which consisted of a single attic room and a shower. All the bedrooms except Lyall's had an unused feel, and he guessed that Lyall had no children, or none that visited and stayed over. Salter descended to the basement and opened all the cupboards until he found what he was looking for, the storage cupboard for Lyall's shotgun. The padlock was still unclasped and Salter checked the cupboard carefully as well as all the drawers in the bench below. Finally he looked in every cupboard and drawer in the basement until he found, tucked away in a bottom cupboard, a box of shotgun shells from which one or two had been taken. He left the house and drove downtown to Lyall's college.

THREE

THE THIRD EARL BATHURST, secretary of the colonies in the early years of the nineteenth century, gave his name to an island and to an inlet in the north-west territories, to a small town in New Brunswick, and to a long street in Toronto that runs north and south through the centre of the city. Bathurst Street once boasted a number of mansions, but it is known today as the street with Honest Ed's on the corner, the famous discount house so successful that its owner now operates England's Old Vic theatre as a hobby. When it was time to find a name for a college to be founded on the depressed downtown section of Bathurst Street, someone discovered why the street had been so named in the first place and decided that it was an appropriate name for the college. Thus, while most Torontonians assume that the college is named after the street, a few know different, and of these a further few show their learning by pronouncing the word with a broad 'A' as the Earl himself probably did.

Although he had driven past it hundreds of times, Salter had never really taken notice of Bathurst College before, because there was no campus as such. It was one of a number of similar non-degree-granting institutes set up in Ontario in the 'sixties to provide alternatives to university education in a time when a fierce spirit of democratization had swept through the educational system, a time when the phrase 'higher

education' began to sound elitist and was being re-
placed by 'further education', a much more embrac-
ing phrase. In the drive to set up as many of these new
colleges as possible before the next election, the government in power had chartered some of them ahead
of their own building programmes, using whatever
spaces were available. Bathurst was housed in a number of old buildings owned by the governments of the
city and the province: a disused warehouse, a nine-
teenth-century home for unmarried mothers, an old
Customs shed, and a synagogue and a church, both of
which had long ago lost their congregations. These
buildings had been refurbished inside, but from the
outside only a small sign on each showed them to be a
part of the college. Among and around them, the
neighbourhood of Portuguese and Chinese cafés and
stores, and the houses of the people who used them,
still survived.

Bathurst, like all the new colleges, was supposed to
respond to its immediate community. It was sited very
close to one hospital and not far from several others
and thus it had set up courses in medical laboratory
technology, and training in nursing and hospital administration. Because it was in Toronto, two other
major concerns were Broadcasting and Theatre
Crafts—lighting, stage carpentry, scenic design and
costume design. Patterns of immigration, the needs of
industry, and just plain fashion continually remade the
college as it tried to respond to every new and tempo-
rary community that took over the area. When it began, it was full of youths of Anglo-Saxon ancestry
taking forms of engineering and business administration, and of their sisters studying home economics.

After that the successive waves of Italians, Portuguese, and, lately, oriental students had taken over the campus for a few years each. The course currently with largest enrollment was typing or 'keyboarding', which was almost entirely full of Vietnamese girls.

Salter drove down Bathurst Street and found a place to park just south of the hospital. He walked a block south and one west, and found himself outside the administration building, a house built by a fur dealer who had guessed wrong about which would be the fashionable part of the city. It had been put to a number of uses since and its transformation into Bathurst's administration building had come just in time to save it from being demolished and the site turned into a parking lot.

He began with the vice-president. He would have preferred to begin with the president, but when he tried to make an appointment, no one seemed to be sure when the president would be in, and knowing a run-around when he met one he chose to accept it for now and settled for Joan Dooley.

He liked what he saw at first: a tall, angular woman with grey, rolled-up hair in a style so out-of-date that she looked as if she had found it in a family album; a neat, dark blue tunic dress and a pair of black loafers all seemed like good signs. Salter explained his presence. 'All the indications are that Mr Lyall was killed by someone robbing his house,' he said. 'But we've had some anonymous letters. Nothing strange about that; we often get them, usually written by a neighbour. I have to check them out, though.'

'What do they say?'

Salter ignored the question. 'I'd like to know something about Mr Lyall. Tell me how long he'd been here, where he came from.'

She put her pencil down and swung to face the window so that she could look at him sharply over her shoulder. Then she swung back and lowered her head, shaking it from side to side, sighing. Then she looked up and shook her head one more time. The whole performance was more appropriate, Salter thought, for a physical education teacher preparing to admonish a ten-year-old girl caught swearing in the gym. Finally, she said, 'Y'know, I told all this to the sergeant who came the next day.'

'I've read the report. He just wanted to know if anyone around here had seen him the day he was killed.'

'And what do you want?' She shook her head again. 'I'm sorry, but we have work to do, too, you know. Aw, heck, forget I said that, but...' She gave three or four more shakes.

'To start with, do you have a personnel file on him?'

'Sure, I guess.'

Salter said, 'Can I see it?'

'Oh, gee, I'm not sure. I mean, a guy's privacy is at stake here.'

Now Salter felt a small gap open up between them, but he waited for her to openly refuse. 'He's dead,' he reminded her.

'So be it, then,' she said, finally. 'Melissa,' she called through the open door to the outer office. 'Do we have a file on Mr Lyall in this office?'

'Of course we do. His personnel file.' Salter heard the girl walk to a cabinet and pluck a file from it. She appeared in the doorway. 'Here,' she said, proffering a thin orange folder.

The vice-president drew herself back and waved the secretary's hand with the file away from her and towards Salter as if the file were unclean. All her actions seemed now too large and too loud, drawing attention to themselves, letting Salter and her assistant know that she was not behaving quite as she would wish.

'I'd like to read this without bothering you,' Salter said, looking around the office.

'There's a chair in Melissa's office, or, no, use the room across the hall. It's the old cloakroom. There's a desk and a chair. Here, I'll show you.'

She led him across the hall and opened the door into a tiny room which smelled of old varnish. 'Not too grand, but . . .'

'It's fine.' He closed the door behind her and settled down to read, skimming the file quickly.

Maurice Lyall had come to Bathurst at the age of twenty-six, and had stayed for twenty-two years. He had an MA in Political Science from the University of Toronto and had begun and abandoned a Ph.D at Wisconsin. Three years before, he had become head of the Social Studies Department. He was married with no children. Apart from this there were three reports by his colleagues saying unequivocally that he was a good teacher.

Salter crossed the hall. 'Not much here,' he said, returning the file. 'Is there someone who could tell me more about him? Who were his friends?'

'I guess I knew him lately about as well as anyone.' She threw herself about in the chair as she talked, lounging elaborately.

Salter saw that her curiosity had overcome her former delicacy. 'There was some evidence that he sometimes entertained a lady. Do you know who he might have been seeing lately?'

'Holy cow! Don't ask me!' She sat up straight in mock horror, her hands on the desk.

'That's the person I'd like to talk to.'

'Well, don't look at me, Inspector. Oh boy, Hah!' She finished in a noisy show of laughter.

Salter remained impassive. 'Any idea who she was? I would think it might be someone in the college.'

'No, sir. Can't help you, I'm afraid.'

'Who can?'

She shook her head. 'You've got the wrong gal for a question like that. I guess I didn't know him that well, after all.'

'According to his file he had applied for the job of Dean of Related Studies...'

'He was just appointed. The interviews were over. He had the job.'

'Everybody happy about that? No bad feeling?'

'I don't think I'd say there was.' She put large, judicial spaces between her words. 'People were pretty frank, but there was nothing personal. Come on, now, Inspector. People don't get killed just because they become deans!'

No, thought Salter. But other people do get spiteful enough to write anonymous notes saying they do. 'Who are ''we''?' he asked.

'The committee. The search committee we set up to find a dean.'

'Does it vote? This committee?'

'Of course.'

Salter took out a pen and a notebook. 'Tell me who was on the committee and how they voted.'

'It was a secret ballot.'

Salter looked out the window, waiting. He could see the roof of the hospital on the next street over and he wondered how his father was doing. It surprised him that just this bit of routine had been enough to keep the hospital at bay for an hour, but now it came rushing back, making him want to walk the streets again.

She shook her head disapprovingly at the way the conversation was going, and sighed. 'I suppose I could make a guess at some of them. Fred Leitch was for him and so was Erroll Czerny-Smith.' She paused. 'I gave the casting vote. He seemed like the best all-rounder of the lot. But, gosh, the others were pretty good people, too.'

Who's arguing? Salter wondered, coming back into the room. He got up and closed the door, nodding into the upraised face of the secretary in the outer room. 'Who were against him?'

'You mean who were for the other candidates?'

'All right.'

'Well, then. My guess would be that Wilf Schreiber was for Jennifer Benson, and so was Shirley Marconi.'

Salter wrote down the names, getting the spelling from the vice-president. 'Two-two, then? Leitch and Czerny-Smith for him, Schreiber and Marconi against.'

'NOT, QUITE,' she said with roaring emphasis on each word, and laughed a lot. 'Don't you dare leave out Gerald. Gerald Pentes was odd man out. He, er, oh hell, he got sore the way he does and voted for David Prince, another candidate. I thought that was pretty—what's the word I want—gratuitous, kinda wild-cardish, because I love David and he's a terrific guy but he's only been around for a year and a half and there's no way he could match experience with Maurice.'

'Were there any other candidates?'

'Jim, of course, Jim Monkman.' She chuckled and shook her head.

'Who got no votes?'

'Waal, I hate to say it but Jim never does. Jim's a hell of a good geographer, but he wants to be an administrator so he applies for everything, and under the rules we have to interview him, but he's starting to look kinda dusty.'

Salter interpreted this as meaning that Monkman must be something of a joke around campus. He looked at the list of names. 'So there were two serious candidates—Lyall and Jennifer Benson, and they got two votes each, and David Prince got one from Gerald Pentes.' Salter looked up from his notebook. 'So, really, Lyall was *your* choice. Right?'

'I *guess* you could say that.' She said it again, more quickly. 'I guess you could say that, sure. But I'd've been happy with anyone they chose. The thing was that Jennifer had no experience of administration, and Maurice had done a cracking good job of chairman.'

'And a split vote means you get to choose,' he pressed.

'OK. It's still a majority, though.'

'What happens now that Lyall's dead?'

'We're just discussing that. Some of the faculty think we should just appoint Jennifer, but the president says the board wants to have a new search, so I don't know. We have to make up our minds pretty soon.'

'How does the process work? You announce the job, put together a committee to look over the applicants, then vote. Right?'

'Pretty well. We get into some real ding-dongs, though, because I like to work for a consensus.'

'But you didn't get one this time.'

'Sometimes the consensus comes afterwards. People think things over and come around to the majority point of view.'

Or they lump it, thought Salter. 'Who appoints the committee? You?'

'No way! The president, or rather the board, appointed one, Fred Leitch. The rest were elected.'

'That sounds pretty democratic.'

'It is, you know. It really is. I think we should run the whole college collegially.'

Salter was not sure what the word meant—like a college?—but there was a defensiveness about Joan Dooley's replies, a note of advocacy which suggested that there might be another way of seeing the process. He would have to find someone else to tell him.

'Where will I find some of the other people on the committee—Wilfred Schreiber or Shirley Marconi?'

'Where are you parked?'

'On Bathurst.'

'It's just that we're spread all over. But I guess you guys don't get parking tickets. I'll get someone to walk over with you. Hang on.' She picked up the phone and dialled, 'Barbara, I've got Staff Inspector Salter in the office. Would you have someone you could spare who could show him the way to the Related Studies building and anywhere else he wants to go? Great. We'll wait for you.' She put down the phone and turned to Salter. 'Barbara is our community relations officer. She's coming down herself.'

Salter walked over to the window that looked over Bathurst Street. 'I don't see any students around,' he said.

'The term's over, and the new one doesn't begin for two weeks.'

'But the faculty are still here?'

'It's part of their contract. This isn't a university. People here work ten months a year. Here she is.'

FOUR

A WOMAN with small black-rimmed glasses and short, slightly greasy dark hair and wearing a grubby, light-coloured raincoat stood awkwardly in the doorway. Joan Dooley introduced them. 'Barbara Czerny-Smith, our indispensable public face: Inspector Salter.'

Salter looked down at his notebook. 'Any relation to—?'

She cut him off. 'My husband. It's still raining a bit. Do you have a coat?'

Salter took his raincoat off the back of his chair, thanked Dooley, and they stepped out the front door.

'Here's a little map of the campus,' she began. 'The Related Studies building is over here. It used to be the head office of a drug company. Where else do you have to go?'

'Someone called Shirley Marconi.'

'She's in that concrete block building over there. Used to be a muffler repair shop. Who else?' She was busy, her tone implied. Salter was being a nuisance.

'I don't know yet,' Salter said, making it clear that he intended to go on being a nuisance as long as necessary.

'Mostly each department has its own building, so you'll find the faculty offices in the same building as the classrooms. But Related Studies doesn't have any students of its own.'

'What is, are, Related Studies?'

'What we used to call the academic subjects: English, Social Studies, Math, that sort of thing. The useless arts, the Commercial Studies' instructors call them.' She took a scarf from her pocket and pulled it over her head. 'I think it's letting up a bit.'

As they walked along Bathurst, she pointed out the college buildings.

'Bit of a mishmash,' Salter said.

A casual remark, but she picked him up on it immediately. 'You mean no painted doorways, fake Gothic towers, that sort of thing? I'll tell you what Bathurst isn't, shall I, Inspector? It isn't a giant education plant with expropriation powers that allow it to blight two or three square miles of downtown Toronto, filling it with educational factories and getting rid of the people who used to live there.' She pointed east to indicate who she was talking about. 'And neither have we built something that looks like a secret weapons establishment in the middle of the tundra.' She pointed to the north.

'So much for the universities around here. What have *you* done?'

'As a matter of fact, we've brought fresh life to the area, to the small businesses. Many of the students have rooms in the neighbourhood and they contribute significantly to the livelihood of the local merchants and rooming-houses. We are very much a part of the community.'

'Like Oxford or Cambridge.'

'As a matter of fact, yes. You find that funny?'

'Yeah, but good too.'

'Another thing. I wanted to meet you myself so you would know to come to me if you need anything. Part

of my job is to look after the college's good name. Can
you tell me why a police inspector is going around
asking questions about Maurice Lyall? We understood that the police were looking for a random killer.
A robber.'

Salter had had enough. As far as he could see he had
done nothing to provoke her tone of barbed defensiveness, and he was in no mood to put up with it. 'I
don't know who you've been getting your understanding from, but until we find the killer, we ask
questions of anyone who knew him in order to find
out anything that might help us.'

'What kind of things?'

'The kind of things police are interested in. Maybe
he was the leading drug dealer on campus, or was in
the habit of sexually abusing his students, as they say.
I don't know. Maybe he offered a student an "A" if
she would sleep with him. That happens, I hear.'

She shook herself as though Salter had flicked some
filth at her. 'Here it is, then,' she said. 'Schreiber is on
the second floor. If you need anything else, you know
where to find me.' She turned and put her face up to
the sky and took off her scarf. 'You remember where
to find Shirley Marconi? Again, as the person most
responsible for preserving the good name of the college and because I personally am very proud of it,
however much of a mishmash it may look to you, I
would be grateful if you would seek any assistance you
need from me. Would you mind?' She strode off
without a farewell before he could edit the obscenities
from his response.

WILFRED SCHREIBER was a political scientist in the Social Studies Department. He was a large, shabby man with wide gaps between very yellow teeth, a huge, sprouting moustache which badly needed trimming, and a bulbous, shiny nose. On his desk was a picture of a large red dog; otherwise his office was bare of any decoration. It might have been a janitor's storeroom.

'Yours?' Salter asked, nodding at the picture.

'My best friend.' He grinned at Salter. 'You are here about Maurice Lyall, I assume?'

Salter nodded. 'Your vice-president has been telling me about the committee that chose him for dean. Those people saw a lot of him lately. You didn't vote for him, I think. You voted for someone called . . .'

'Jennifer Benson.'

'The vice-president didn't think she had much experience. Why did you prefer her to Maurice Lyall?'

'Because she didn't want the job as badly as Maurice Lyall did. You should never have administrators who really like their jobs.'

Salter, the sometime administrator himself, said, 'You want the place run by amateurs?'

'Oh yes, certainly. The whole place should be staffed by amateurs, especially the faculty. Never trust professionals in education.' He smiled. 'I'm an anarchist,' he said.

'I thought you must be something. A professional anarchist?'

'Touché, and up your ass, Inspector.' The grin stayed in place. 'I've got a perfect alibi,' he added. 'It was my twin brother who did it.'

All the signs were already there. Schreiber spoke for effect, epigrammatically, if he could get the words in place in time, an artifice Salter associated with a certain kind of academic, always dispensing bon mots to a tutorial, even when there were no students around. Salter suspected that the students would hold Schreiber in high regard for his style, associating it with the television plays they had seen set in old European universities. He also suspected that Schreiber would always prefer to speak even when he didn't know anything. He felt himself in luck.

'Tell me about Maurice Lyall. I've read his file. When was he separated from his wife?'

'About ten years ago. What's this all about?' He leaned forward. 'You think someone here killed him?'

'We think he was killed by someone who broke into his house, probably intending to rob him, but there are one or two things that don't quite fit.'

'Such as?'

'Let me ask the questions, Mr Schreiber.'

Schreiber leaned back and smiled. 'What can I tell you?'

'Did he have a girlfriend?'

'There were rumours.'

'Could you lay that out a bit?'

'No, I couldn't. There was gossip but you'll have to ask someone else who the lady was. I don't know.' Schreiber looked pointedly away from Salter.

'What does that mean?'

'It means I don't have any gossip.'

'How about if she killed him?'

'I still don't know who she is.' The message was clear. Schreiber knew, and he could not resist showing Salter that he knew, but he was taking this opportunity to show that he was a man of principle.

'Is that why you wouldn't vote for him? Because he was screwing around?'

'No, no, no. That had nothing to do with it.' Schreiber climbed down from his moral perch. 'I don't care who he slept with. I voted against him because he was on his way up the ladder. He wanted to be a dean because he regarded it as a promotion. Now that is very bad for the college...'

'Isn't it a promotion? Being chairman or dean?'

'Yes, but it ought not to be. It ought to be something you do because your colleagues insist that it's your turn in the barrel. At the moment it's the other way round. The point is that if it is a promotion, then returning to teaching is a demotion, a loss of face, so the incumbents do everything to stay there, especially the deans, or get promoted some more, and pretty soon the place is run by a caste of administrators who spend their time talking about the problems they are having with the faculty.' Schreiber was talking faster now to get his aphorisms out as Salter looked at his watch. 'So whenever I'm on a selection committee I make it a rule to vote for the candidate who least wants the job.'

'In this case, Jennifer Benson.'

'Yes. I was tempted, mind you, to vote for that young lad from the Theatre Department, David Prince. I know nothing about him but he hadn't the faintest idea how the college worked, which I thought a recommendation. But I had to go for Jennifer to stop Lyall. Didn't work, of course. Our vice-president recognized Maurice as one of her own, just as I did.'

'Was there anything really wrong with Lyall?'

'Yes, there was,' Schreiber put on an air of deep seriousness. 'This is confidential. He was my chairman,
you know. I didn't realize how far things had gone
until I happened to glance at next year's timetables
that he had left on his desk. He had put himself down
for a single class on municipal politics, but there was
another timetable marked "chairman". You see what
that meant?'

Salter shook his head. 'Something bad, eh?'

'He *knew* he would be dean. They had already
anointed him!' He roared out this revelation in mock
impatience that Salter hadn't seen something so obvious.

Salter wondered how Schreiber defined gossip,
guessing that the teacher confined his scruples to not
tattling about the sexual lives of his colleagues. 'So
they won?'

'They *always* win. Otherwise they wouldn't be
where they are, don't you see? But if you know what
they're up to you can sometimes put a spoke in their
wheel for a little while. They nearly fumbled it.'

'How?'

'I don't know yet,' Schreiber adopted a reflective
posture. 'To start with, they had their lackey, the assistant registrar, Fred Leitch, and Gerald Pentes and
Shirley Marconi, against me and Czerny-Smith, so it
looked good for them from the beginning. Then
Pentes threw a tantrum and without him it was two-
two. So, smelling trouble, our vice-chairman ad-
journed the meeting. Then Shirley Marconi obviously went sour on Lyall, so it was three-one for us,
which was how it went, with one abstention. But
Leitch had set this up, and he pointed out that an ab-

stention rendered the vote invalid. So we met again, and this time Czerny-Smith switched to the administration's side and it was back to two-two again, with Joan Dooley holding the casting vote. We'll get them one day.'

Salter concentrated on trying to memorize the names of the chief players. 'Why is Leitch on the committee?'

'Leitch is the administration's appointee. The assistant registrar. We never had an assistant registrar before—we only just got a registrar—because the accountant used to do it all, but Leitch was parachuted in one day and work was found for him. Political connections. No mystery there. I don't think he'll be around very long because he has trouble comporting himself in a way appropriate to a college, even this one. When he first met the lady who is the chairperson of Secretarial Science he asked her if she would agree that no secretary is permanent until she has been screwed on the desk, and was surprised when she didn't laugh. There have been a number of complaints about him since. The real mystery is Czerny-Smith—' he paused to underline the name '—elected by the people to vote for Jennifer, and turning traitor. He wouldn't discuss it afterwards, and hasn't since.'

Salter looked at his notes. 'Are you telling me that this Jennifer Benson was the choice of the faculty?'

'No, I'm telling you that Maurice Lyall *wasn't*. In fact Jennifer was a last-minute choice. She makes many people uneasy—she's very far left—but we couldn't find anyone else.'

Salter said, 'I've just been told that four members of the faculty are elected to the committee, and one member is appointed by the administration, in this case, Fred Leitch, and that these proportions are all laid down.'

'Yes, it was all settled about five years ago. In a report of a special committee of the administration and the faculty. The—' he added quickly in case Salter thought he was finished— 'Schreiber Report.'

'You wrote it?'

'I chaired the committee. We wrote a report which, if they adhered to it, would solve all their problems, but they continually go behind it, and now it has something like thirty-six amendments.'

In a minute, thought Salter, he's going to explain the stupidity of those amendments, one by one. 'Then why doesn't the faculty get the person it wants every time?' he asked.

'Two reasons. First the faculty are never united. It's like Republican Spain, all splinter groups who don't trust each other. The administration don't have that problem, of course, so they can usually exploit our rifts. In this case it was known that Shirley Marconi disliked Jennifer Benson, so the administration thought it was sitting pretty. But then she went sour on Lyall for reasons best known to herself—and perhaps to the late lamented Maurice—and so with her vote we should have got Jennifer until Czerny-Smith changed his mind. The second reason is that your information isn't entirely accurate. It's true that four are elected, but only three are elected by the faculty, and one, Gerald Pentes in this case, is elected by the department chairmen as a group. Now the department chairmen are a group of upwardly mobile junior administrators who tend to elect someone on the side of order, the side they've just joined. So the truth is three are elected by us, one is elected by them, and one is appointed by them. I know what you are going to say, we still have a majority, but then you get a wild card like Shirley Marconi and we come apart. And if we don't, the board, which has the power of veto, thinks such a split is divisive and tells us to start all over again and try and find a consensus. Heard that word much yet?'

'And Pentes had a tantrum.'

'He's got a very short fuse, has Gerald. I gather he found a moral lapse in the way the administration handled the process and got on his high horse, even though he was put on the committee to vote for Lyall. He's famous for taking umbrage.'

There was more to come, and Salter waited.

'He's known as "Say-it-ain't-so-Joe". You remember, after Shoeless Joe who took a bribe to throw the World Series and there was a young boy when he came out of the hearings, saying, "Say-it-ain't-so-Joe." Our Gerald has spent his working life being appalled, disgusted and generally upset at the continual discovery that all men are liars, even or especially around here.' Schreiber switched into a more normal conversational voice. 'He's a bit silly, to tell the truth, and the administration should have had more sense than to put him on the committee. Still, it backfired on them, so that's all right.'

'What about this other candidate, Monkman? The vice-president said he always runs for these kinds of jobs.'

'I have a theory about Monkman. I believe he hopes that one day he'll get one vote in a deadlocked situation, and he'll be able to convince one of the front-runners that he could throw his vote to him, the way the big boys do, in exchange for favours after the appointment. He hasn't had any luck yet. He may be waiting for them to put students on the committees.' Schreiber's glee indicated that he didn't believe a word of this.

'But you voted for Jennifer Benson,' Salter cut in.

'Yes, she's got a wicked tongue, and she's not tactful, so we would have had an uproar in a week, but she is on the side of right, a reluctant candidate.'

'Who persuaded her?'

Schreiber dropped his derisory stance. He looked at Salter warily. 'I did, as much as anyone. A number of us. It wasn't hard. Jennifer said that Maurice Lyall was on the make from the start.'

'So she could count on your vote, no matter who else applied for the job, the way administration could count on the assistant registrar's vote for Lyall?'

'Barring the appearance of Jesus Christ himself, yes. It's different, though. We're the good guys: they're the baddies.' Once more he was grinning with pleasure at the ironies that were piling up.

Salter felt he had heard enough academic politics for the moment. 'What sort of reputation did Lyall have with the students?'

'As far as I heard, he was a good enough teacher...'

'Sexually,' Salter said.

'That's blunt. I never heard of anything. No charges of harassment, nothing like that.'

Salter folded his notebook. 'That'll do for a first run through.'

But Schreiber wasn't finished. 'The only one we haven't discussed is our vice-president, the chairman of the committee. Have you met her? Of course you have, she's the one who explained to you how democratic we are, and told you how we voted on the secret ballot.'

'She seems very competent.'

'Did she tell you that she didn't understand why she has the job, why she ever let us talk her into it, how she can't wait to get back to teaching? No? She will. She makes a point of saying it to everybody. She came from a teacher training college in Alberta to run our staff training programme. A lot of the faculty came here with no background in teaching and no formal training, and instead of seeing that that was an advantage, one of our former presidents decided we ought to have a staff training officer, and Joan Dooley got the job.'

'How did she get where she is?' Salter didn't much care, but he was learning a lot in the interstices of Schreiber's monologue, mostly about Schreiber.

'She floated there by sheer natural ability. We had some trouble a few years ago when the part-time teachers went on strike and set up a picket line. The board wanted to fire them, and some of the rest of us got our organization to send a letter of support—' here Schreiber grinned once more—'we didn't actually join them on the line, of course; our duty to our students came first, not to mention our pay cheques—what actually happened was that two courageous full-time teachers booked off sick to avoid crossing the picket line and the rest of us—including me—got up a petition—but what I was going to say was, in all the skir-

mishing, somehow Joan Dooley bobbed up calling for
a healing of wounds and got made go-between, and
then the mediator, and when the dust settled, accepted the job of assistant to the president to advise
him on human relations, and in no time at all became
vice-president.'

All this was delivered in a tone of rollicking mock-
ery; the pleasure that Schreiber took in being able to
deliver some obviously much-rendered observations to
a new audience took some of the edge off his deliv-
ery, but there was plenty of malice left.

'This was Lyall's department,' Salter said. 'Which
was his office?'

Schreiber opened the door and pointed out to the
larger office outside where several instructors shared
a communal space. 'At the far end,' he said.

'The room with the door open?'

'Yes, the concept of private offices hasn't taken
hold at Bathurst yet. The chairman and one other—
me, at the moment—get their own rooms because
that's how the space was divided when we took the
building over. This building used to be an abattoir. I
imagine that the chairman's office used to be the
slaughterer's and I have the book-keeper's, something like that. But it's understood that if our less for-
tunate colleagues have to talk privately to a student
they are free to use either this one or the chairman's
when we aren't here.'

'You don't lock them?'

Schreiber smiled. 'No, nor do we usually leave anything interesting around for our colleagues to look at.
They are just work-places.'

FIVE

SALTER DECIDED HE WANTED to know the backgrounds of these people before he went any further, and he returned to Joan Dooley's office with a request for some more personnel files. She waved him towards her secretary, who retrieved the folders and Salter retired to the room across the hall where he spent some time reading and constructing a story, a history that contained all the names and dates he wanted to remember.

THE DAY'S ACTIVITIES had achieved their purpose of keeping the misery and the fear at bay, but though he took the absence of messages as a good sign, he did not much want to go home. When he got there he found that May was at the hospital where she intended to stay. 'I went down there to bring her home for a meal but she wouldn't leave him alone,' Annie reported. 'Eat your supper and I'll drive you down. I made Swedish meatballs so that we won't be living on bacon and eggs. If you find yourself on your own you can slice them up for a sandwich.'

'What's the trouble? Is he bad?' Don't dodge it now you're here, he thought. Keep asking to know the worst.

'I just called the hospital. They said he was restless.'

'That's their language for telling us he's in agony. Did you see him when you went down?'

'No. Sit down. Have a beer. This'll be ready in a minute. Then take an hour on the couch. If you stay at the hospital you won't have much of a night.'

'I have to. It's the only way she'll come home.'

'I know.'

He waited until nine o'clock, then Annie drove him down and waited in the car for May. 'They want six dollars an hour to park here,' she said. 'What do poor people from Barrie do when they have a sick relative here? Take out a bank loan?'

Salter took a quick look at his father who was muttering loudly with his eyes closed, then went in search of May. He found her in the waiting-room at the end of the ward, trying to catch a nap on a hard little two-seater bench. 'Go home,' he said. 'You can't do any more good here. I promise you I'll call if there's any need,' he said. 'You can't do any more good here.'

'A woman who was just here said that last night she heard someone calling for a nurse for two hours. This man was calling very quietly, but she could hear him from the waiting-room. When she couldn't stand it any more she went along the corridor and he was in the room next to the nurse's station where three of them were looking at wedding pictures. When she asked him if there was anything she could do he asked her for another blanket. Thought she was a nurse. He felt cold. Now, be fair, they knew he couldn't be cold, look how hot it is in here, so they hadn't bothered. But he *felt* cold. I'm not having your father lying there calling out all night and no one bothering.'

'Go home, May. Get some sleep. Come back as early as you like, but go home now. I'll stay until you come back.'

'You have to work.'

'I'll be all right.'

'You won't go away?' This was her real concern.

'I'll be here until you get back.'

'Maybe I will, then. I am a bit bushed.'

'Annie's waiting across the street. I'll come to the door with you.'

At the front door, she stepped back. 'I've got no milk,' she protested. 'I must get some milk.'

'You're staying with us, May. Remember? We've got plenty of milk.'

BACK IN THE HOSPITAL he braced himself for the first session. It was eleven o'clock. He saw how the night would go. He had a bundle of magazines that should take care of the first two hours without much fuss. After that there would be another hour of reading in snatches, and then the intervals between looking at his watch would grow shorter and by four o'clock there would be nothing left in the world that he wanted to put into his mouth—tea, coffee, soft drinks, mints, even a Mars bar—he would have tried them all, and his tongue would be like a bedsock and each tooth would have a little jacket of felt, the whole experience like crossing the Atlantic by plane at night.

He took off his tie and loosened his shoes and picked up the first magazine, thinking even as he did so that he ought to be able to go into a trance or slip on a loin cloth and stand on his head or even just *think* the night away if he were better trained and belonged to a different culture, and then the idea of a major distraction crossed his mind, something that would keep him busy for an hour or two, and he put on his shoes and went out to Bay Street where he found an all-night grocery and bought a pad of writing paper and a ballpoint in case his own ran out, then, remembering his vision of the night, a toothbrush and some paste as well as a cup of coffee and a Kit Kat. He returned to the hospital, passing a bum in the doorway who had just been patched up in the treatment room, giving him a dollar, and made himself as comfortable as he could in the waiting-room. There was a small desk, used during the day between two and four by a hospital volunteer who helped anyone who needed help between those hours, and here he put his writing materials and composed himself to write.

His idea was to use the time to begin a report on the Lyall homicide, not an official report of an investigation, but, rather, since no one was watching, a narrative of the day's reading and interviews. Should anyone surprise him by looking over his shoulder, he could say he intended to draw on it later for the official report, if one was required, but in truth he was projecting the most private of activities, keeping a journal.

He found it incredibly difficult to begin. *I was assigned the case on June 4,* he wrote, then thought: Who cares? He tried again. *After looking over the scene of the crime, I next visited the campus of Bathurst College.* He threw the page into the garbage can. The problem was he was still writing a report. He tried to imagine a different audience than the deputy chief of police. After several more tries he addressed his wife, imagining her absent, in Turkey, say. *Dear Annie*, he wrote. *I am sitting in the waiting-room of the hospital. It is now twelve o'clock and I thought I would fill in the time by telling you about this case I'm on.* This was better.

Young Lyall was a bit of a radical by all accounts, he began. He unwrapped his Kit Kat, ate it while he thought about his next move, then settled himself to his task again. He took off his shoes and loosened his belt a notch. When he returned to the paper, something had happened. Whether it was the time of night or the circumstances, he felt a desire to write it as well as he could; he had become a critic. Early in his very brief university career a professor had returned an essay he was proud of marked 'Vague fine-writing', and this so stung him that he had sweated over every phrase in his next essay for that instructor. The result had read like an Anglo-Saxon chronicle, but there was nothing vague or finely-written about it.

He looked at the last sentence and started again. *Lyall began life as a radical,* he wrote. Better still. He laid down his pen and thought of getting himself some more tea from the machines in the basement. At this rate he would probably write ten sentences a week. On the other hand, an hour and a half had passed in a flash. He would get some tea and start properly.

Half an hour later he re-read his first sentence and continued. *When he first came to Bathurst he taught everything in the Social Studies Department as required. Lyall was very popular, and was voted 'Teacher of the Year' in his second year. After a few years he became interested in the teachers' union,*

*taking on different jobs until finally in 1984 he was
chairman of the local.*

*Then for two years he was on leave, first on a paid
sabbatical, then on unpaid leave, trying to get a Ph.D.
He never got it, though, and he came back to Bathurst to teach in the fall of '87. In that first year he was
also in charge of Social Studies in the extension programme (night school), then in 1988 he became chairman of the Social Studies Department, a job which he
held until he was appointed Dean of Related Studies.*

*Set out like that, it's an old story, isn't it, Annie? A
young man, full of piss and vinegar, wants to change
the world, then, very often through the trade union,
gets to like being a manager, and then becomes ambitious because it's better than working for a living, in
this case teaching, and partly because that's the way he
is. In Lyall's case, the union started him off, but I
think it was the little job in the extension department
that showed him what he wanted to do, and sent him
on his way.*

*When the time came, Lyall was ready. He applied
for the job as Dean of Related Studies and got it, after some interesting shenanigans. Then someone shot
him. Who? Why? The chances are that he was killed
by someone he knew. It's a slight possibility, of course,
and there's nothing to back it up, or there wasn't until we got some anonymous letters, more or less telling us to look on the campus for the killer.*

*So far I've established that they might have come
from the college. The notes were printed on an IBM
laser printer, using standard computer paper. There
are thirty-seven such printers in the college and they all
use the same paper.*

I interviewed two people today, the vice-president, Joan Dooley, and an instructor named Wilfred Schreiber.

The vice-president seemed to me at first like a Girl Guide leader, all camp-counsellor language and wanting to see the best in everybody.

Schreiber, an instructor I talked to later, made it clear that he thought she was—what? a phoney, I think, and I have my doubts about her, too. She speaks well of everybody, but that's just a style she's adopted. Still, Schreiber, who I'll come to later, has to be taken with a pinch of salt, too. I think at the moment that Joan Dooley would be amazed to learn that anyone didn't find her genuine. She thinks she is. That she was on the opposite side to Schreiber on the committee doesn't mean much until I know more about the people involved. Schreiber thinks the vote was rigged, but he has no idea how. All he says is that Lyall knew he was going to get the nomination. There are a couple of interesting things about the process that will become clear when I've talked to the others on the committee, but at the moment, as far as I can tell, first, Lyall could have lost, even if he was the administration's choice, and second, Joan Dooley had a perfect right and reason to cast her vote for Lyall if she thought he would be the best man. None of the others sound like much, except one called Jennifer Benson.

I'm glad I met Schreiber early in the game because I think I'll be going back to him. He's a talker, and he likes to be in the know. The shrewd analyst is how he sees himself. He calls himself an anarchist, thinks he understands everyone including himself, but he strikes

me as someone so keen to have his insights appreci-
ated that he would advise the president, too, if he was
asked. He's like one of those pundits you see on tele-
vision on municipal election night, giving their opin-
ions on what the early results mean. I think, ideally,
he'd like to be consulted by the power boys, but until
then he'll offer his opinions to everyone else.

Here Salter paused to see if he was repeating himself, decided he probably was but that the repetition
was justified on the grounds of rhetorical emphasis.
Besides, he felt himself on a bit of a roll, and he liked
the shape of the last few sentences. *'Fact is, Schreiber*
doesn't have a good word to say about anybody, and
now that I think of it, he could just be jealous of Joan
Dooley.

He voted against Lyall. He's got some bullshit the-
ory that you shouldn't have anyone in administration
with any experience, but it all comes out so smoothly
that I think he made it up ten years ago and has been
reciting it to visitors ever since. He loves to hear him-
self talk and he's going to be useful if this goes on
much longer. If I get any sleep at all tonight, I'll start
on the others tomorrow.

More than three hours had passed, and he had done
what he could. He put the pad inside a magazine and
tucked the magazine into his small pile of reading
material. There were no disturbing sounds along the
corridor—some moaning from one room, and the
noise of an elevator opening and a stretcher being
wheeled out. He was tired now, and he walked quietly
along to check that his father was asleep, then let
himself into the room with the stretcher and managed
to spend four hours with his eyes closed. But before he

went to sleep he reversed the journal to start again on the clean back page. At the top, he wrote, 'My father may be dying and I don't know what I'm supposed to do. No, I don't know what I'm supposed to *feel*. I know how I *do* feel. As if everyone's watching me. But about him? I didn't think we were that close. I feel now as if I'm about to let him down, as if all the times I've done it before are piling up on me. I feel as though it's my fault. He makes me feel that way. He always did.' He stopped, exhausted by the effort to be honest, and embarrassed by the result, closed the notebook and slipped it inside the magazine.

He woke up to find a small black nurse standing over him, grinning. 'Talking in your sleep,' she said. 'All about your girlfriends, you disgustin' fellow. Want some breakfast? I've got some extras, one with porridge, one with Rice Krispies and one with All Bran.'

'What happened? Those three die in the night?'

'Don't you be being cheeky now. I always order extra. Now do you want one or not?'

'I'll take the Krispies.'

She put the tray on the coffee table and Salter took a spoonful of the Rice Krispies, but they were still the same as he remembered from twenty-five years before and he settled for a cup of warm coffee and some jam on a slice of old, cold toast.

He brushed his teeth in the washroom and went to see his father. May had arrived without noticing him, and when Salter walked into the room she was helping him drink some tea.

'I took the subway down,' she said. 'Annie was still asleep when I left, so I thought I'd leave her.'

'Thank God you've come at last,' his father croaked, apparently recognizing him.

'He's been here all night,' May said. 'Now drink your tea.'

'Couldn't have been. He'd have had this lot arrested.'

'Why?' Salter asked.

'I'll tell you later,' May said, trying to cut him off.

'All night,' the old man repeated.

'What?'

Blushing slightly, her voice lowered, May said, 'He's been hallucinating again. He thinks that the nurses have been assaulting the patients and ... having sex with them.'

'In the corridors. All night. Fighting and humping,' the old man confirmed. 'They shouldn't allow it, should they?'

'Who does he think I am?' Salter asked May.

'He's been going on about his brother Fred.'

'Fred was killed at Dieppe in 1942,' Salter said.

'He's been going back before that, to when you were kids.'

'Not me. Him and Fred.' He turned back to his father. 'I'll have it stopped.' To May he said, 'I'll call in at noon.'

'I'll be here.' May took a towel and started to wash his father's face, and Salter left.

SIX

HE STOPPED AT HIS OFFICE to get a shave and to report on what he was doing, then drove back to Gibson Avenue and let himself into Lyall's house, wanting to poke a little more deeply into Lyall's nest, to arm himself with a sense of the kind of man Lyall was.

He adopted a circular progress, intending to end in the centre at Lyall's desk.

The tiny garden was no more than a grassy space for some outdoor furniture, with an empty flowerbed running along beside the fence, waiting for a real gardener to take over the house. The basement (the next circle) was simply a storage area: apart from a rack of skis, both cross-country and downhill, and a pile of ski boots under the rack, the only thing of interest was the gun cupboard, which was the one part of the basement that had been built by a skilled carpenter. The rest of the shelves around the walls had been slapped together out of scrap lumber. The ancient workbench was covered with odds and ends—a single hinge, two old towel racks, and a dozen assorted tools. Lyall, Salter concluded, had been a sportsman but not a handyman.

He moved to the ground floor and established quickly that Lyall was no cook, either, and that he did not expect to be surprised by hungry guests. His fridge held orange juice, milk and half a loaf of bread. An ancient packet of lima beans shared the freezer compartment with a frozen trout. There was nothing to indicate that he did more than assemble his breakfast here; there was not even a list of frequently-called numbers beside the telephone. The living-room at the back of the house also had an unused feel, like an old-fashioned parlour.

In the attic room on the third floor, a bureau was half full of the kind of clothing usually left behind in summer cottages—old sweaters and thick woollen socks. The closet was bare. The next circle, the guest bedroom on the second floor, had silted up slightly with the detritus of Lyall's past, outdated ski-ing clothes that a wife would have got rid of, thermal underwear, and two curling sweaters.

Lyall had kept all his current wardrobe in his bedroom, including the 'good' ski-clothes. But though closet and bureau were crammed, the bedroom seemed otherwise bare. Beside the queen-size bed was a table, a lamp, a clock, and a copy of *The Times Educational Supplement.* On the other side of the bed there was nothing, not even a table. Clearly, no one was expected to stay the night.

At the very centre of all the circles was the study, the room where the real Lyall must have spent his life. Salter began with the desk, reading everything on its surface and in the little wicker tray, looking for names of people Lyall had met recently, finding nothing except utility bills and offers from book clubs. His desk calendar contained only self-explanatory appointments or impenetrable memos.

He opened the drawers in the left pedestal and picked his way through Lyall's bank statements and the evidence that Lyall was beginning to dabble in investments. Looking over a month of Lyall's affairs at random, Salter was impressed by the size of Lyall's salary. The second drawer contained an old typescript, evidently an attempt at a novel, and the top drawer was full of all the equipment and supplies needed in an office.

The right-hand pedestal contained a single cabinet full of personal files, labelled without system; 'Correspondence', for example, 'Income Tax' and 'Published Articles'. Salter flicked through the files, then turned to the main filing cabinet, a four-drawer affair in the corner of the room, but the labels on the drawers showed them to contain the material of Lyall's discipline, chiefly his teaching notes, and Salter decided he was almost finished. Before he left the study he ran the tape on Lyall's answering machine, listening to the messages of the last three weeks. Most of them were routine—confirmation of a doctor's appointment, messages from the college—but through the tape ran a thread of a woman's voice, never identified but recognizable after the first two messages: 'Hi. Call me this evening between eight and ten;' 'It's me. I can't make it;' 'I'll call later.' Salter ran over the tape until he thought he would recognize the voice if he heard it again, put the reel in his pocket and drove off to Bathurst College.

HE MAPPED OUT A ROUTE for himself, listing everybody he had heard of so far. He began at the former muffler repair shop with Shirley Marconi, the committee member who had switched her vote away from Lyall.

'Can we do this outside?' she asked. 'I'd like to smoke.'

They left the building and crossed the street to a Portuguese coffee-shop. He bought them some coffee and they took it out to the sidewalk where there was a single small iron table and two chairs. She lit up, shuddering slightly in mock repulsion at her addiction. She was thin, with black hair cut straight, without make-up. Salter placed her in her mid-forties.

'Did you know Mr Lyall well?' he began. 'I'm trying to find his friends to get an idea what he might have been doing that day.'

'Moderately.' She pulled the corners of her mouth wide and down in a wry grimace. As they spoke, she contorted her expression continually to give her words some drama.

'Were you in favour of him as dean?' Salter asked.

Her eyebrows shot up. 'I wouldn't have voted for him for dog-catcher.'

'Why?' What did he do to you?'

'He never came near me. It was what I observed that made me sure that he ought not to be in charge of other people.'

'When did you observe it? After you were elected to the committee?'

The face stopped working. Then, after several seconds, she said, 'I understood that the proceedings of the committee were confidential.'

'Not if someone gets killed.'

'All right. I found out during the interviews.'

'Something he said. Or did?'

'Something he did, but not during the interviews.'

'What? What did you find out?'

'That he was quite unsuitable.' She swung her head violently, first to the left, then to the right, to emphasize the last two words, then lit another cigarette.

Even though he was primarily killing time, Salter was growing bored with this. 'It'd be a help if you'd tell me why. Did you learn of some extraordinary tendencies you hadn't been aware of? Did he call you up and offer you money to vote for him? It's not that big a college. You've been here for twelve years. Didn't you already know all about him?'

'Apparently not.'

'So what did you find out?'

'That he was ruthless, ambitious, and sexist. And I don't consider myself a feminist.' Finally, a qualifying statement.

'Did he make a pass at you when he found out you were on the committee? That would cover all three. Miss Marconi, I didn't get much sleep last night, and I'm investigating a homicide. What did you find out? Tell me something to wake me up. What was wrong with him?'

This produced another sentence. 'I found out that he threw people away.'

Salter sighed. 'What does that mean?'

'What it says.'

'Who did he throw away? A woman, of course.'

'It was just a general remark.'

'Who?'

She shook her head.

'Does everyone know why you voted against Lyall?'

'They know exactly what you know. Will you stop this ridiculous questioning? All that happened was

that I found out, realized during the interview, that
Maurice Lyall was unfit for the job.'

'So you voted for Jennifer Benson?'

'Yes.'

'Why?'

'Monkman is ridiculous. And David Prince is a
child.'

'How did you feel when Lyall got the job?'

'I was so angry I rushed right over to his house and
shot him.'

'Two weeks later.'

'Was that it? I forget.'

Salter tried for a casual remark. 'Will Benson get the
job now?'

She stared at him. 'I haven't the faintest idea. Nor
do I care. I told you, I'm not a feminist. Lyall
did . . . was the kind of man who damaged people's
lives, people more valuable than he was.'

This was better. Salter dipped his spoon into the
mud at the bottom of his cup. 'That bad? Damaged a
lot of people?'

She saw the trap. 'As far as I know, he didn't swin-
dle anyone, or physically abuse them. He was simply
the epitome of a certain kind of person. I'm in no way
implying that he had enemies here who would go to
the lengths you're suggesting. All I meant was that a
dean . . . deals in the careers of people, and what we
don't need here is a dean who is concerned only with
himself.'

She was talking at last. It was time for the hard
questions. 'Miss Marconi, from the cleaning lady and
from other sources we know that Lyall had a girlfriend. So far everyone I've asked has acted kind of

coy, but I intend to find out who she is. You can see how important it is for me to get some idea of Lyall's habits. I want to know where he was that day, who he was with, who he might have been expecting. It was a holiday, just the kind of time you wouldn't expect someone with a girlfriend to be on his own. If he wasn't with her, she still might be able to tell me why. I need to know if he was in the habit of keeping a gun in his bedroom at night. And lots more she might be able to tell me. Now, am I talking to the right lady?'

'Me? You think I was his girlfriend? Good Christ. I thought he was a total creep.'

'But you were going to vote for him in the beginning, then you changed your mind because of something he did to someone. Who? I'll get there eventually. There'll be a phone number in his diary. The neighbours will be able to describe her, or her car. It's hard to park on that street. But I don't want to waste any time. Who is this woman?'

'This is incredible. I said nothing about any woman. All I said was that I learned something of the kind of man he was and you are inventing a whole I-don't-know-what out of it. I made a character assessment, that's all.'

'After twelve years?'

She looked away, then rammed her cigarettes into her purse and stood up. 'I have a class.'

There was nothing more to be got from her at the moment, but she was obviously concealing something out of loyalty to whoever Lyall had damaged. He would come back to her when he had an idea of who that was. In the meantime, she did not seem to have any reason for sending anonymous notes.

His next interview was with Erroll Czerny-Smith, the French teacher. According to Salter's notes, Czerny-Smith had also changed his mind during the committee's proceedings, but in his case in favour of Lyall.

Without a guide he had some trouble, for none of the students he asked seemed to have heard of him, but he found him eventually behind a door marked 'Language Laboratory' seated at a console at the end of the room. Salter launched into his prepared speech about there being 'one or two things' which were at odds with the assumption that the killer of Lyall had been a casual robber. The purpose of this form of words was still to catch a flash of recognition from one of them which might hint at the authorship of the notes, but once again, Salter got no answering gleam.

Czerny-Smith said, 'I'd had nothing to do with him for the last ten years, so I can't tell you a thing about his private life.'

'And before that?'

'Before that we were friends. Close friends, once.'

'What happened?'

'Nothing. We didn't have a fight, or anything like that. The friendship wore out. We got on each other's nerves.'

'Did you vote against him, then?'

Czerny-Smith pursed his lips and pretended to tidy his desk. 'It's a small college, Inspector. I've had three phone calls about you already. So I know you know how I voted.'

He was about fifty, nearly bald, but with a fringe of bright silver around his ears and on the back of his head. All his clothes were slightly too tight, indicating that he had only recently acquired the layer of fat around his neck and was perhaps hoping to take himself in hand before he was forced to buy new ones.

'So why did you vote for Lyall?'

'Because I thought he was the best man for the job, of course.'

'Did you start off thinking that?'

Now the teacher looked less happy. 'I may have said something in the beginning about preferring Jennifer, but that was just thinking aloud. I thought she was impressive, yes. But as the process continued, I overcame my doubts about Maurice and decided that he was the better person. All right? Can I get on now?'

Salter watched him try to shuffle the single sheet of paper on his desk. 'You must have been happy when he was appointed, and now you've got to go through the whole process all over again. Who will get it, do you think?'

'No one has told me we are going through the whole process again. As far as I'm concerned the job belongs to Jennifer.'

Salter said, 'I was just talking to Shirley Marconi. It's a bit weird that she went the other way. She says what she realized during the interview was that Lyall was the *wrong* man. Sounds as if you were at different interviews.'

'The process is bound to be somewhat subjective.'

'But it sounds like you interviewed two different people,' Salter pressed. 'Until the interview, she liked Lyall, and you didn't. Then you both flipped. But you've both known the man for years. What was it about him that impressed you at that point?'

Czerny-Smith flushed, 'There was no one thing, for Heaven's sake. An interview is a pressure situation, and I thought he behaved well under pressure... What is it?'

The door had opened and Barbara Czerny-Smith was standing in the doorway. She stood waiting with an awkward air, seeming to have left her abrasive manner outside.

'This is my wife, Barbara,' Czerny-Smith said. 'Staff Inspector Salter.'

'We've met,' Salter said. 'Hi, there.'

She ignored him. 'I won't interrupt. It's the luggage keys. I couldn't find them last night. Do you know where they are? I want the key to the big black suitcase.'

'In the bowl on my desk.' He did not look at his wife.

'Can I have the door key? I can't find mine.'

Czerny-Smith took a key from a ring and held it out without rising from his chair. Salter leaned over the desk and took the key, handing it back to Mrs Czerny-Smith.

'Where will you be?' she asked.

'You can find me here. Are we finished, Inspector?'

'Right.' She waited a few more moments, but when he looked away she turned to Salter. 'I just had a message for you. Judy Kurelek would like to speak to you.'

'Who's she?'

'She's an instructor in the English Department. She says you know each other and she wants to say hello. I'll wait outside and point you in the right direction.'

She looked back at Czerny-Smith. 'In the bowl on your desk,' she repeated. He did not look up.

'Anything else?' he asked Salter, when she had gone.

'Not for the moment.'

It was evident to Salter that he had just been witness to a scene from a marriage in trouble, if not completely on the rocks, and that if he pressed further he would probably become the focus of Czerny-Smith's misery. He would come back.

SEVEN

JUDY KURELEK ran a writing workshop on the second floor of a former knit-wear factory. Salter was beginning to be impressed with the way further education could be conducted within the cast-off buildings of a departed industry. The room was large enough to have held ten or fifteen knitting machines. The machines were gone but the tables had been planed and sanded to make writing surfaces, each one big enough for two students. Near the ceiling, the original fans were still revolving; the only obvious additions to the old factory were the rows of lighting tubes suspended over the benches.

Kurelek worked out of a small glass-walled cubicle in one corner of the room, the office of the supervisor of the original sweat-shop. Salter tapped on the open door and watched Kurelek look up and pretend surprise. 'Inspector Salter,' he said. 'I got a message. Seems we're old friends. Can I come in?'

She jumped forward to place a chair, then closed the door behind him. 'I was trying to be discreet. You are the policeman investigating . . . ?'

'I'm inquiring into the death of Maurice Lyall,' Salter agreed. He recognized her voice immediately; it was the woman on the tape in Lyall's study.

He watched her make a decision, and then look squarely at him. 'I understand you feel it's important to know who Maurice's girlfriend was. It'll save time, I suppose, if I tell you. Does this have to be public?'

'I don't see why, yet.'

'Well then, we were seeing each other.' Now she made another decision. 'I believe very few people knew about me and Maurice, but evidently word has leaked out that he had someone, so shall we establish where I was on that Monday night? I was at a cottage near Honey Harbour, on Highway 69, about two hours' drive from Metro. I went up there on the Friday to help some friends open up the cottage for the season, and I came back at first light on Tuesday morning. I got home around nine and I had a class at eleven.' She wrote on a slip of paper. 'Here. Here's the address of the friends I stayed with, and here's the name of the service station where I left a flat tyre to be fixed at seven in the morning.'

It was hard to guess at Kurelek's age, probably in her forties. She was dressed in the kind of costume that Salter realized he had seen about a lot and was probably therefore out of date and (thinking sexist and ageist?) a little young for her—a black sweater over skin-tight leggings and ballet-type shoes. In the corner of the room a shiny black mackintosh hung on a peg. Like a witch, Salter thought, but on the other hand Kurelek seemed to give off such a healthy aura that the tiny whiff of perfume he had caught was an incongruity. She looked as if she should smell of coal tar. A healthy witch, then.

Salter put her card in his pocket. 'What can I ask you about Maurice Lyall?'

'Whatever you like. We were lovers, until he ran for dean. Then we weren't. Surely it doesn't matter? The

word around here is that he was killed by a vagrant
trying to rob him.' She held his eye firmly and spoke
more loudly than necessary, as if Salter were an aero-
bics class.

'That's the most likely. We have to look at everything, though. Why did you stop being lovers?'

She said, 'Does that mean you think someone
around here did it?' When he didn't answer, she
seemed to brace herself before she resumed. 'I...liked
him. He was unthreatening to women—to me, anyway, and I thought at one time that it might come to
something. It never did, though, because he didn't put
enough energy into it. He wasn't looking for a grand
passion so we didn't find one. He was more interested
in his job than he was in his private life, but we got
along. We went out to dinner and so forth, but in the
end he was a bit undeveloped emotionally.'

'What does that mean?' Salter wondered if the
phrase could be applied to him.

'It means not being much interested in anything except your career. No music, no books, no travel, no
hobbies, even. Appetites are something to be satisfied
while you're thinking about something else. Meta-
phorically speaking, it means steak and the missionary position. I find most ambitious people are like
that.' She paused. 'Including my husband.' She was
quickly becoming comfortable, though her natural
mode seemed to be the slightly artificial formality of
someone dealing with a class of students for the first
time. She had had some time to think since, apparently, Marconi had called her, and what Salter guessed
he was getting now was the prepared response. The
words, the stance, everything, had been run through

at least once, probably to her friends to account for the break-up of the affair. The graphic reference to 'steak and the missionary position' was intended to evoke an image of greasy lips and bouncing loins, to shock him slightly with its sophistication, put him off his stroke.

'Why did you stick around?'

She laughed slightly. 'Missionaries can be very good at what they do.' Another polished line.

'So why did you break up just then?'

She leaned forward and dropped her voice, adopting a conversational tone, changing the dynamics between them: it was a chat now, between old acquaintances. 'We didn't break up. That's the wrong term. We stopped sleeping together, that's all.'

'When?'

'A couple of weeks before he was killed.'

'You didn't stop seeing him altogether?'

'We had lunch one more time, I think. We never used to have lunch at all because people see you and talk, but it didn't seem to matter as long as there was really nothing for them to talk about.' She stopped and looked through the glass wall out to the factory floor. 'It's a funny thing, on that one lunch date I realized what I really wanted in the first place was...intimacy, but not necessarily sex. I don't think adultery is always about sex any more, not for women, anyway; of course, that's what the word means, but... but I decided I could manage without him.' She stopped and faced him, forbidding him to comment on her digression.

But Salter was left wondering if even this bit of wool-gathering had not been rehearsed. 'Who left who?'

'It was mutual.'

Salter was finding it difficult to believe Shirley Marconi's interpretation. Surely even in a college it was all right these days for a man and a woman to make out, as long as no one else got hurt? Then the missing piece of the puzzle came into view. 'You are married.'

'What does that have to do with it?'

'You live with your husband?'

'I do.'

That would do it. No one wants a home-wrecker as a dean. Be a nuisance. Salter made a note to himself, then asked, 'Did you spend much time at his house? How did he live? His cleaning lady says there was a silver tray missing.' He consulted his notebook. 'And they seem to have taken his watch.'

'Ah yes. The one the Spanish Railway Company gives away for riding on their crack train—the Andalusian Express I think it's called. Maurice got one when he went on some conference last summer. I can't describe it except that it's black with a little blue and yellow emblem on it, I think. And the name of the railway. Would you like some coffee? I can make you some.'

Salter looked across at the shelf containing a bottle of instant coffee and some powered milk. It had always puzzled him that apparently well-brought-up people could drink such stuff and call it coffee, when it was just as easy to pour water through some grounds. Mixing coffee dust, powdered milk and hot water seemed to him justified only during a siege. And now here was another one who apparently did it every day. 'Sure.'

After she had handed him his mug, she said, 'Did they get the money? He kept a lot of money in a drawer. Perhaps as much as two thousand dollars. He held a garage sale, and he sold some books to a dealer—quite a lot of stuff. What he called a Mexican New Year, when you burn everything you own and start again. I saw it when he paid me some money he owed me. In twenties, I remember. He was born poor and he still got a kick out of a thick wad of actual money, so instead of putting it in the bank he kept it in a drawer and filled his wallet as he needed. Did the thieves get it?'

'Probably.' He made a note and sipped his coffee, setting it aside immediately. It tasted as if it had been mixed with dried blood. 'Can you describe the tray?'

'Georgian. Worth about three thousand dollars. Maurice didn't go in much for antiques but I think he bought this tray for someone else and then kept it.'

'How big?'

She made a circle with her fingers. 'The size of a dessert plate. Where did they break in?'

'They didn't. Just walked in.'

She nodded. 'He kept money in a drawer and he never locked the doors, and he used to brag about that. A perfect set-up. Did you find any finger-prints?'

'Dozens. We don't know whose, though. Did he go hunting much?'

'Hunting? Oh, you mean the gun. He was the only academic I've met who did. He was from Manitoba.

He grew up shooting ducks. I don't think he shot anything bigger.' Now they were into the questions she hadn't prepared and he watched her picking her way through any implications before she spoke.

'Did he hunt still?'

'Earlier this year he went up to Tobermory with a group he'd picked up with. I think they were just practising.'

'At that time of the year, they would have to be. Did you know where he kept the gun?'

'It wasn't a secret. In a cupboard in the basement.'

'Did you ever see it?'

'He showed it to me once. Very phallic, I thought.' An attempt at a little joke. 'What happened? Did they find it first?'

'We don't have the answers yet. You say you broke up with Lyall because he was ambitious. You mean the dean thing?'

She shook her head decisively, back to the dialogue she was ready for. 'Oh no. That was just coincidence. If that hadn't come along, it would have been something else.'

'Did he talk to you much about the job? Did he expect to get it? How badly did he want it?'

'Very badly. He had enough votes, he thought, but he and I had parted before the final count. You know about all that switching around at the end. Everybody else does.'

'More or less.' There was still the thread she was avoiding that he wanted to catch. 'So he didn't break up with you just because he was running for dean?' he persisted.

'No, I told you. It was mutual.' She looked angry but sounded much less certain. 'What are you saying?'

'I'm not saying anything. It's what I'm hearing from you. He was ambitious, he applied for the dean's job, then dumped you. I thought maybe you'd become a problem.'

She looked at him for several seconds. 'Somebody else said the same thing. And now you, an outsider, come along and that's the way it looks to you, too.'

'Who was that?'

She shook her head.

Salter said, 'It wasn't just backbiting? Someone who didn't like him?'

'No, it wasn't.' Now she was trapped into defending her unnamed friend. 'I happen to know she was one of his supporters until...'

'Until he dumped you.' He pretended to look through his notebook. 'Was she on the committee?'

'Yes.'

'Shirley Marconi. She's very loyal, isn't she? Wouldn't tell me who you were, and phoned to warn you I was coming.' He picked up his coffee, then put it down again. 'When did you tell her Lyall had dumped you?'

'He didn't dump me!' She pulled a paperclip straight. 'At least, I didn't think so at the time. If he did, then he did it very well. Shirley thought so because she never liked him. She was looking for a reason to vote against him. But would anyone... dump someone, just to get a job?'

'Your friend seems to think so.'

'God! Well, I didn't, not then.'

'I'm sorry to have to ask you this, but do you know if he took up with anyone else after you two separated?'

'He only had ten days.' She shook her head. 'I had lunch with him on the Tuesday before. We were civilized, I thought. He made a joke about how much work bachelors can get done. Quoted something by Kant, something vulgar about... about keeping the body quiet so one could work. I was meant to understand that his days and nights were now given over to work.'

Suddenly she stopped being an interviewee. 'Is it possible?' she asked. 'Would *you* give someone up, just to get promoted?'

'The question wouldn't arise,' Salter said. Uxorious, he thought, that's me, especially this afternoon. Then, because his reply had sounded priggish, he added, 'What I mean is, the question of someone telling me that if I wanted a promotion I would have to give someone up. You see...'

But now she did see. 'If you and Shirley are right, then I'm glad he's dead.'

EIGHT

HE HAD TIME to round up the last remaining members of the committee, leaving the disappointed candidates until next day.

Fred Leitch, the assistant registrar, was, as Schreiber had described him, a creature of the administration. 'My job was to deliver Maurice Lyall as dean,' he told Salter. 'Which I did.'

Salter asked him if he had been aware of any bitterness when Lyall was appointed. 'Oh, sure,' Leitch said. 'That Marconi woman wanted his head, God knows why. And that dickey-bird who taught History, Pentes, was in some kind of snit right from after I approached him.'

'About what?'

'I understood he'd been put there like me to vote for Lyall, the way Schreiber and Czerny-Smith had been put up by the faculty to vote for the Benson woman. Shirley Marconi was the loose cannon. When she seemed to be favouring Lyall, I thought it was in the bag and I said so to Pentes. Christ, he hit the roof. Started screaming at me about integrity and sacred trusts, all that shit. What the hell did he think the administration had elected him for? I thought I'd screwed up royally, then Czerny-Smith switched and we had it again. But I'd lost track of it all by then.'

'Why did he switch?'

'You tell me. Found his soul, it sounded like. Who can tell with these dinks? As I say, the deal was, he was the faculty's boy, in there to vote for the Benson woman, and that's the way he acted, right up to the last days. Then he suddenly started talking about the importance of experience—Lyall was a chairman, see—and consulting his constituents. If I were running their union I'd make sure who was on my side. But this is academic politics. You hear a lot of talk about academic politics being rougher than the game I used to be involved in up at Queen's Park. But it's not, you know. You can't trust anybody, is what they mean, and you know why? Tenure. These suckers can't be got at; they've nothing to lose, so you've got no hold over them. "Rough" is when the guy who stabs you in the back takes a chance.'

Last came Gerald Pentes, historian. A carefully-brushed little man with thinning, wavy fair hair and half-glasses which he took off for the interview. He was abnormally courteous, which put Salter on his guard because it did not seem to be the natural way of a gentleman but an affectation of courtesy, as if Pentes had pressed his 'courtesy' button and might have others that he could press just as easily. And so it proved. For five minutes, while they were discussing what Pentes knew about Lyall (almost nothing, it turned out) the historian acted as if Salter were a student who had told Pentes he liked his classes, and then Salter asked him if he had intended to vote for Lyall initially—'I know how the vote went in the end,' Salter added.

Pentes went mad. 'This is *exactly* what happened on the committee,' he said, his voice, his whole body, trembling, and his face flushed except for the end of his small pointed nose, which was white as if from frostbite. 'I find it completely unethical that knowledge which is supposed to be confidential is bandied about in a way to make it clear that the whole process is utterly suspect.'

'What process?'

'The vote. How did you know who voted for whom?'

'They told me.' Salter pointed over his shoulder. 'Everyone I talked to.'

'Words have ceased to have meaning. The ballot is supposed to be *confidential*.'

'It's OK to say afterwards who you voted for, isn't it? If you want?'

'Of *course* it isn't. Obviously if you know how everyone except one person voted and you know the result then you know how that one person voted and the vote is no longer confidential.'

Salter thought he had never seen a greater disparity between an event and the reaction to it. Pentes was trembling so hard he seemed on the verge of a seizure, triggered by what seemed a very minor cause.

'I gather you voted for Mr Prince.'

'Since you seem to know and have no doubt told everyone else, may I know who else voted for whom among the others?'

'Sure.' Salter consulted his notebook. 'Schreiber and Shirley Marconi voted for Benson, and Leitch and Czerny-Smith voted for Lyall. The chairman of the committee voted for Lyall. At one point you could've been kingmaker.'

Pentes said, 'I had no interest in being kingmaker. Are you sure Czerny-Smith voted for Lyall? And Marconi for Benson?'

'If you voted for Prince, yes. You sound surprised.'

'Since you know everything else, I'll tell you why. I thought it was the reverse, that Shirley Marconi was in favour of Lyall, and that Erroll would vote for Jennifer Benson.'

'Someone said that everyone changed their minds in the course of the interviews, like you. Musical chairs. Why do you think the others did?'

'I haven't the faintest idea. Perhaps they didn't like to be taken for granted, either.'

Salter waited.

'It's perfectly true. I did favour Maurice in the beginning. Then their henchman Leitch talked as if he and I were hired by the administration to vote the way they wanted, and that made me very angry.' He looked away, shaking his head. 'So corrupt,' he continued. 'The sort of thing you read about but never expect to experience yourself. Not in an institute of higher education, at any rate.'

Salter looked out the window at the used car lot next door. 'So Leitch's pitch with you backfired.'

'I decided then that if Maurice Lyall was their candidate I would oppose him. I thought he was the best man but it seemed wrong to let Leitch's gang win.'

'He got there in the end, though. Why didn't you vote for the woman? That would have done it.'

Pentes pursed his lips into a tight knot. 'She's a fanatic who attacked me once for the material on my course. If she were dean she would be completely disruptive. I don't want to say more.' He lifted his chin up and away to dignify his silence.

AFTER SUPPER ANNIE drove him to the hospital to relieve May, who still refused to leave her husband unattended. After he had got May into the car, he went for a walk over to Yonge Street and bought himself some coffee to begin his vigil.

He returned to the ward an hour later to find his father lying almost naked on his side, the covers pulled back, his nightshirt around his waist. His father was a modest man, from a class and generation that never went in for family nudity, and Salter had never seen him exposed before. Now someone at the hospital had casually stripped away the old man's dignity, baring him to the world. Salter stepped to the door of the room and called down the corridor to the nursing station. 'Nurse,' he bellowed to a blue nylon overall. 'You! Here. Quick.'

The woman looked up from the stack of paper in front of her. 'The nurse will be along in a minute.'

'Now!' Salter shouted, and started to walk towards her.

Three other women in different coloured nylon gowns looked up. All of them seemed to be working their way through a pile of documents. The finger of responsibility rippled round the circle and stopped back at the first woman in the blue gown. 'What's the problem?' she asked, still without moving.

Salter paused in his progress. 'Come and see.'

They looked at each other for several moments before she gave in. She came down the corridor and looked at his father, leaned forward, twitched down his nightshirt and put the sheet back over him. Then she looked at Salter to hear what the problem was.

Salter said, 'How long has he been like that?'

'Like what?'

'Naked and freezing.'

'Well, come on...'

'WHO WAS THE LAST PERSON TO LOOK AT HIM AND WHEN?'

'I just came on. I imagine he's been receiving treatment.' She called down to the nursing station. 'Is 654 receiving treatment?'

One of the women called back. 'I think I saw Melanie come out of there. Getting a blood sample.'

'When?'

'About half an hour ago.'

Salter said, 'Does Melanie plan to come back?'

'She's up on the seventh now.'

'How long would he have stayed like this if I hadn't come along?'

'There's no need to shout.'

'Yes, there is. There's a big need to shout. I came to visit my father who is suffering from a number of things including the care he's getting around here, and I find him bare-ass naked, cold, and not even a goddam curtain around him. There's a big need to shout.'

The nurse gave the sheet an additional twitch. 'I just came on,' she said.

Salter gave up. 'So how is he?'

She looked at the clipboard again. 'He's stable,' she said. 'Receiving treatment.'

He wondered if she were doing it deliberately. 'How is he?' he asked again, his voice rising again. 'Who's in charge of him? Is he better than he was yesterday? Will he improve tomorrow?'

'I'll get Dr Cheng to speak to you.'

It took two and a half hours, but eventually an exhausted-looking Chinese resident appeared and told Salter that his father was progressing satisfactorily, and that the time was coming when Salter ought to be thinking of moving him to a convalescent hospital. Salter thanked him for the advice, knowing what May would say.

In the waiting-room, a small, pinched-faced woman in her sixties huddled in the corner with a knitted woollen coat pulled tight around her. 'I heard that,' she said. 'You have to keep right on top of them. When I came in this morning I found my mother lying there with a big swollen hand. One of the nurses' aides told me she'd found her, half an hour before, tied to the bed. When she found her, my mother's hand was black. You got a smoke?'

'Sorry. You can't smoke here, anyway.'

'Can't you? Worried about your health, are they?' She got up and wandered down the corridor, spoiling for a fight.

BY TEN O'CLOCK the ward was quiet, and Salter prepared for the night. He had carried about with him all day a big envelope containing his writing materials and toothbrush, and now he set out his coffee and the packet of Hob Nobs Annie had provided him with.

I saw the rest of the committee today, he wrote. *I'd still like to know who wrote those notes.*

Shirley Marconi has a good name—she seems wired all right . . . He paused. *Smokes like a—'* he tried to

avoid the cliché—*people used to... Nice outline but
hardly any flesh—no ass to speak of—and a face just
short of being a skull. When the committee first
started meeting, she was all in favour of Lyall, then she
says she found out he was 'ambitious, ruthless, and
sexist'. So she switched and voted for a 'fanatical
feminist' instead. So what did she learn? As far as I
can tell, that he just broke up with her pal.*

Erroll Czerny-Smith was the next. A wimp. He
paused to ponder whether a two word sentence was
allowed. He liked the feel of it and decided to make
that his chief guide. He continued. *Czerny-Smith used
to be a pal of Lyall's but they grew apart, and he
planned to vote for Jennifer Benson. Then he changed
his mind. Why? Because he couldn't stomach Benson? He seemed pretty glad she was finally getting the
job. Maybe when the crunch came he just found that
he had to stay loyal to his old pal. His wife is the college PR officer, and they're having a fight. Why?
Anything to do with the way he voted? My impression was that he was the angry one, she the one who
was sorry. She seemed to be yearning a bit towards
him in the office, trying to be agreeable, not at all the
way she'd been with me, but he wasn't having any.*

*I enjoyed Fred Leitch, the assistant registrar, lackey,
tool of the bosses (this is Schreiber's version). On the
whole the people in this place are not too different
from those I encountered at Douglas College when the
English teacher was murdered.*[1] *They all seem to need
to polish everything they say. So it's a relief to meet a
real foul-mouthed hard-ass like Leitch. I knew all*

[1] *The Night the Gods Smiled.*

*about him from Schreiber, and I half expected to find
that the guy making the sexist jokes was a sleaze, but
he isn't that. He's a survival-of-the-fittest character,
the kind whose time is probably coming. I doubt if
he's trained himself to eat dead rats, but he admires
the guys who do. But he had no possible interest in
sending anonymous notes, and they certainly aren't
written in his style. He's thinking about his next job
and how much he can sue the college for, if he can get
them to fire him.*

*The last one was Gerald Pentes who is a bad case of
integrity mania.*

*Tomorrow I'll talk to the other candidates, most of
all to the Benson woman.*

*This is a good thing to do, because by writing the
above I've calmed down a bit. Tonight I found him
lying in his crib, balls to the breeze, like a giant baby,
and I got a little uptight. It wasn't just the incident that
upset me. It happens. I just can't get comfortable with
what I'm supposed to do about all this. It's guilt, Annie says. She thinks I think I haven't been very good
to him these last twenty years, and now he may be dying, and I'd like him to go in peace. With me in peace,
she means.*

He paused long enough to have some second
thoughts. *Fact is, I realize now what was going on. I'd
had the first good day since he came in this place, going round interviewing those teachers. But as soon as
I started for home it all came back. I feel so sorry for
the way the old bugger looks, lying there in a bed full
of nightmares. I wish he'd get better so I could forget
about him. But I didn't want to come down tonight,
so when I came in and found him looking abandoned*

I had something easy to do. Throw a fit. Did me good, too. Made me feel useful.

I haven't done much for him for the last twenty years. Annie's done her best, having him over every month, but it's always an ordeal. He still won't refer to her by name—calls her 'she' and 'her' when he's talking to me. I don't think it's all my fault. We're just not that close. So why am I having such a bad time? Seth seems to get along with him, so at least he's made friends with his grandson.

'YOU'RE MR SALTER?'

Salter lifted his head from the desk where he had fallen asleep. It was two o'clock. Standing across the desk was a nurse in a white overall. 'Yes.'

'I've brought you a cup of tea. Drink it and go home. Your father's comfortable now, and I can hear him if he stirs. There's nobody else in the other bed in his room. He'll be all right.'

Salter wiped the drool from the corner of his mouth. 'When I came in last night—' he began.

'I know. I heard.' She cut him off. 'He'll be all right now.'

Salter sipped his tea and believed her.

'Have a look at him on your way out,' she offered.

Twenty minutes later he let himself quietly into his house. All the beds were occupied, so, not wanting to disturb Annie, he stretched out on the couch in the living-room under an old duvet.

HE WOKE TO THE SOUND of voices in the kitchen. May was talking to Annie. 'He's so proud of Charlie,' she was saying. 'Tells everybody how well his son's do-

ing. Even asks the local policemen if they know him.
I tried to make him see that people grow away from
each other, but he knows people who see their fami-
lies every weekend. That's why it'll be good if Charlie's there when he wakes up properly.'

'Seth has been around a lot in the last couple of
years,' Annie offered.

'He used to say he gets along better with his grandson than with his son. I told him to count himself
lucky. Seth's a special sort of boy, isn't he? He and
Seth used to go for a walk sometimes, round the
neighbourhood, and he'd show the boy off to everybody, proud as anything, but he always introduced
him as "My son Charlie's lad".'

Christ, Salter thought, I don't need this. He turned
over and tried to shut out their voices.

A little later Annie tiptoed into the living-room and
put her finger to her lips. May came downstairs and
Annie took her straight through the front door to the
car.

When she returned an hour later, she said, 'You
were awake. You heard most of that?'

'All of it.'

'The news at the hospital is a little better, and now
is not the time to talk about it, anyway. But if you
want to talk about it later, we can. In the meantime,
don't crucify yourself.'

NINE

AT BREAKFAST he tried to get caught up with his family. Annie told him that Seth, his younger son, was auditioning for another role in a television play.

'He seems to be doing all right,' Salter offered, tentatively.

'He's getting work, which is what it's all about. The fact is, your son is a nice kid and it comes through on camera.'

'And Angus?' Their elder son was presently in Prince Edward Island, working for Annie's family business.

Annie smiled and set up the coffee machine before she replied, 'Linda is pregnant. Six months pregnant. They just decided to tell us.'

'Yeah? Hey. A grandchild? Which would you rather, a grandson or granddaughter? Hey, but...'

'They're going to get married.'

'So you'll be a grandmother. You don't look like one.'

'I feel like one.'

'So do I.'

'A grandfather?'

'A grandmother. Don't go away.' He reached for her, lecherously. But the joke and the gesture were only a cover for his failure to control the muddle his emotions were in. 'You'll be late for work,' he said, holding on to her.

She laughed. 'That was the wrong thing to say. Haven't you noticed? I haven't been to work since he went in to hospital.'

'You've been looking after May. And me. I'm all right now.'

'You're starting back, maybe. But you're not all right.'

'I'm all right.'

'Is it very dreary down there, waiting? You want me to come down there when you're there? For a while?'

'No, no.' Salter paused, wondering whether it would sound silly. 'I've been keeping a journal.'

Annie thought about this for a minute. 'About you and your father?'

'What? No, about this case I'm on. It makes the time pass.'

'Can I see it?'

'Not on your life. I'm not about to watch you correct my grammar. Well, maybe. I'll see. Why did you think it was about me and Dad?'

'I thought maybe you were trying to get straight how you felt about him.'

'I don't have to write that down. It's simple. I haven't done much for him while he's been alive, and I don't want him to die before I've told him.'

'Told him what?'

'That I'm sorry.'

'That'll make you feel better. You think it will cheer him up?'

'What are you saying?'

'Nothing. Not a word.'

'Come on.'

'All right. What I think is obvious, but someone said once that life consists of finding out that platitudes are true. Or was it clichés? Anyway, I think what's done is done and the record isn't all that bad. Do what you want, do what you have to, but there's a difference between feeling bad for your father and feeling bad about yourself. So be careful and try to think what's best for him. That's all.'

'Say that again.'

She repeated it, nearly word for word.

'You think I'm being selfish?'

'That's the wrong word. I think it might not help him to hear your confession. Right now, *do* everything you can. Leave the rest until later.'

Salter took this in over several sips of coffee. 'I'll give it a try,' he said, finally.

'What about this case?'

Salter looked at her, puzzled, until he realized she was changing the subject, then told her about his day at Bathurst.

'Are you serious?' she wanted to know. 'I mean, it doesn't sound as if it really grips you.'

'It passes the time. Call it therapy. Fact is, there's a lot of soap opera stuff going on, you know, a lot of politics and drama about nothing much. Someone up there is stirring it up, sending anonymous notes. I'd like to know who.'

'What time is your next appointment?'

'I don't have one. I'll just drive down and go through the rest of the list, the other candidates. Tell you the truth, I intend to spin it out. It's a lot more entertaining than writing a report on gambling, or waiting around that goddam hospital.'

Annie came behind his chair again and slid her hands down his chest, hugging him. 'I don't have to rush off, either. How about giving old Granny a tumble, after all.'

Was she just trying to cheer him up? He turned in his chair and reached up and kissed her, guessing that would be the end of it. 'Now?' he asked.

'Would you rather have a rain check?'

'The sun just came out.'

'Then let's call it therapy.'

THE MOST OBVIOUS other person to talk to was Jennifer Benson, the formerly unsuccessful candidate who everyone agreed had been Lyall's only serious rival.

Salter found her at her desk in the Commercial Studies building where she taught English as a Second Language to recent immigrants. She was a short, heavy woman in her early forties, without make-up and with fair hair chopped short and pulled back in two clips over her ears. Her door was open and Salter's first view of her was of a very large bottom as she bent to struggle with the wheel of her chair. She straightened up, puffing, and shook herself.

Salter told her he was simply ticking off names, hoping to pick up anything that might tell him something about Lyall.

She said, 'I thought everyone was assuming that it was a thief, maybe a pair of thieves, who got interrupted. Just a statistic.'

'That's the most likely.'

'If not, then someone around here did it. I'm the most likely, and it wasn't me.' She hooted briefly, then apologized. 'Sorry, but I didn't like our Maurice.'

'Why?'

'Why?' Why didn't I like Maurice?' she asked herself rhetorically. 'Let me see. There was a time when Maurice Lyall was what they call a prominent faculty spokesman. But we elected him once to the Board of Governors to look after our interests and in no time at all the pig became a man. That's why.'

'Why did he do that?'

'The appointed members of the board scratched him behind the ears and he rolled over and put his trotters in the air.'

'So you decided to go up against him?'

'Somebody had to. I didn't give myself much chance, but our side had to have someone to vote for.'

'You must have thought you had it wrapped up when Shirley Marconi moved over to you.'

'God, yes, wasn't that something!' Again she honked with laughter. 'If they had voted then I'd be dean now, giving everybody fits. But Erroll came through for them, so that was that.'

'Did he tell you why?'

Now Benson lost some of her glee. 'No, he didn't and I don't understand that, and he must be ashamed. We go back a long way, and I've always thought he was a bit of a wimp, but he's been on the side of right. The left, that is. I thought he was mine no matter what. But something turned him around. I think I may have gone too far in the interview. If I was trying to get the job, I mean. But, you know, I never thought I had a chance, so I told them what I thought, really thought.'

'About what, how you would do the job?' Salter relaxed, enjoying her. It was difficult to see Jennifer Benson writing poison notes, or firing guns.

As she recalled the day, she grinned again at the memory of the fun she had had. 'Everything. I started with the women's issues, of course. They expected that, but I went a little farther than they expected. I went on then about the academic standards. Fact is, I'm really very conservative. Even my feminist friends get frightened when I suggest someone else should be grading their students' papers. Maybe that's where I lost Erroll? That's what it was. Yes, I said a lot of things that I believe about changes I would make if I got the job, and looking back now I guess I scared him. I think that's what happened. On the other hand, maybe they bribed him. Let's wait and see what kind of car he buys.' Again she roared. Then quieter, 'Or if he runs for chairman.' She paused. 'Vote for Lyall, and he'll support you for the chairman's job.'

'Is the job open?'

'Not for another year. But it's nice timing.' She looked thoughtfully at Salter, then shook her head. 'Nah, he's a wimp, not a sleaze.'

'He and Maurice Lyall went back even farther than you and him, didn't they?'

'Yep. But they came to the place where two roads met a long time ago. They haven't had much to do with each other for a few years, then nothing at all when Lyall's wife left him. Yes, Erroll and Maurice were pals, and then they weren't, and I'm pretty sure that there was a reason why Erroll voted for him. He'd been *got at.*' She pronounced the phrase with comic melodramatic flourish and nodded heavily in confirmation of her thoughts. 'But how?'

'How much did you have to pay Shirley Marconi for *her* vote?'

She looked up, startled, then laughed and scratched her head with a pencil. 'Now there you have me. I thought Shirley hated my guts. She and I don't exactly see eye to eye. Question is, what did she suddenly have against Maurice? The only conclusion I can come to is that our Maurice tried to get her vote lying down and that would be a bit blatant even for her.' She smiled. 'I think he tried to screw her, but all he did was screw himself. Forget I said that. And then there's little Gerald. Geraldy-Weraldy Pentes. The administration thought he was their boy, which he was, but someone was stupid enough to tell him so and they ran up against his principles. Silly people. Honestly, they deserve to have Jim Monkman as dean.'

'They've got you now, haven't they?'

'It looks like it, doesn't it? I wonder if they can find a way round it? Probably.'

Salter got ready to leave and asked the question that had been on his mind since he arrived. 'I've seen you before, haven't I?'

'Possibly. Were you one of the ones on horseback? Look me up on your computer. If you can't find me, ask the Mounties.'

'What for?'

'I'm a protester,' she said with the air of one declaring herself a member of the Flat Earth Society, making fun of herself before anyone else could. 'I've protested nuclear disarmament, the Vietnam war, Free Trade—you name it, I've marched. The Mounties must have twenty pictures of me. We got quite fond of one of them, invited him to a farewell party when our chief protester moved to Vancouver.'

'Did he come?'

'Sure. I expect he got permission. A nice lad. I used to know your first wife,' she added slyly. 'We marched together.'

'But mostly you're an English teacher.'

'That's right. I only protest in my spare time. Mostly I draw a big fat salary for helping refugees learn enough English to become capitalists.'

'Like Schreiber.'

'No, not like Schreiber.'

THE LAST TWO, James Monkman and David Prince, took Salter only a few minutes each.

Monkman, the geography instructor and perennial candidate, was, without doubt, the best-dressed man on campus, in a grey tweed suit, an Irish linen-looking shirt and a wool tie. He was in his mid-fifties with grey hair, sparse on top, but thickly waving down the back. His accent was impenetrable. At times Salter heard cockney, or was it South Africa? At other times there seemed to be some Welsh. Salter settled for somewhere in the Commonwealth whose accent was unfamiliar, like Bermuda.

Monkman cleared up his doubts immediately. 'I did a spell in your lot, Staff Inspector,' he said. 'Hong Kong, actually. Just for a year or two.'

'You were born there?'

'No, no. I went out there straight from university.'

'From England?'

'New Brunswick, actually.'

'You're *Canadian?*'

'Not by birth. Came out when I was sixteen. Went to UNB, then to Hong Kong, then came back when that folded.'

'Where did you go to graduate school?'

'I didn't. I got my feet under the table early here, so I'm permanent without that. I was hired to teach a course for security officers, but it never got off the ground. So I switched to Geography. I could have taught pretty well anything they offer here but I know geography, more than these kids, anyway. I've knocked about a bit and the kids like my anecdotes.'

Salter said, 'What do you think happened to Lyall?'

'He got himself shot by a couple of lads who were using Fireworks Night as a cover,' Monkman said promptly. 'What's your intelligence like? Got a wire into the Vietnamese gangs?'

Salter nodded. 'Nothing to do with being made dean?'

'The thought never crossed my mind.'

'What about women?' Salter was inviting Monkman to join him, one policeman to another.

'I haven't heard of any. I wasn't a pal of his, though.'

'What happens now?'

Monkman looked surprised. 'You'll have to talk to the neighbours, won't you. See if anyone saw anything suspicious.'

'I meant here, about the job he got.'

'Ah. Yes.' Monkman sat up a little straighter. 'They'll have to choose one of the other candidates, I should think, wouldn't you? They can't go through the whole process again. Take them six months.'

'Maybe you'll get it this time.'

'If experience counts, I should have a good shot. I've been in administration all my life until I came here. That young actor is still in diapers, and there's only the Benson woman, a real ball-breaker.'

Salter thought, not for the first time, that it was impossible to overestimate a man's good opinion of himself.

'What happened last time? Do you know how they voted?'

'It's a secret ballot, of course, so you can't be sure, because they really don't breathe a word about how they voted, but Schreiber told me privately I had handled myself well in the interview, and Leitch and I see eye to eye, so I'm pretty sure I must have come close. I doubt if anyone voted for Benson.'

DAVID PRINCE DID NOT LOOK like an acting instructor. In his black knee socks, striped tie and Madras jacket, he looked as if he had something to do with money. When he found that Prince had never even met Lyall, Salter was even briefer with him than he had been with Monkman.

'It seems early days to be applying for the dean's job,' Salter said. 'Did anyone encourage you to apply?'

'There was a notice posted. Anyone could apply. So I did. Of course I didn't expect to get the job. I just wanted to see how the system worked.'

'What happens now? Will you leave your name in?'

'Oh, sure. I got a vote this time. Maybe I'll get two next time. Or if someone shoots the other candidates,

I'll be the only one left.' A tiny smile broke through Prince's youthful deadpan.

Salter stood up and put his notebook in the brown envelope. 'How did you get into teaching?' he asked as they went through the door.

'The usual way. I graduated from drama school with an MFA—that's Master of Fine Arts, by the way, not what it looks like—' another tiny smile—'spent a year discovering that I can't act, so I decided to teach. I can do that all right, but I think my future lies with administration.'

ALTHOUGH SALTER HAD some idea of which one was more likely to know what had actually happened in the committee room, the signals he had got from Monkman and Prince were so different he thought it worth seeing if Schreiber could throw any light on them. He found him in his office, eager to be consulted.

'Had a chat with Monkman and Prince,' Salter began. 'You know, I've been getting a different understanding from everyone about how the vote went.'

Schreiber rattled off the score again.

'None for Monkman?'

Schreiber paused for several moments, then looked slightly embarrassed. 'Jim thinks someone voted for him, did he?'

Salter said nothing.

'You must know what happened, what always happens.' Schreiber paused to close the door, and continued in a lowered voice. 'I'm afraid that Jim Monkman hasn't a snowball's chance in hell of getting an administrative appointment, here or anywhere else. He's the idlest man on campus, a former policeman, you know—' he opened his mouth and bared his teeth to show he was being humorous—'and fools nobody. On the other hand, there's no need to be rude to his face, so he never hears the truth. When he comes to me, after it's all over, and tries to pump me in the most pathetic, hopeless way—I don't think he could have been a very good interrogator—I remember he's a human being and try to think of something kind to say. Now Jim, being who he is, is easily able to translate my soothing remarks into solid support, a vote, maybe two. I'm not guessing all this. I was told by several people that he thought he had my vote and one other. It's embarrassing and hard to counter because the vote is supposed to be secret. On the other hand, it's harmless because just about everyone who cares knows what happened. You said Prince, too. Is he under the impression that there is a huge underground movement going for him?'

'I got the impression that he about guessed it right.'

'Did he? I never spoke to him afterwards. Well, well.'

TEN

SALTER HAD thought through Annie's comments at breakfast to some effect and decided that all-night vigils were not serving any purpose. After an early supper he planned to relieve May at the hospital, then stay only until the ward quietened down.

Annie said, 'I'll drive you down and bring May back. Do you mind getting the subway home? I promised May I'd take her over to her apartment and fetch some more clothes. Then I thought I'd catch a movie. I need a night off.'

Seth said, 'I'll come with you, Dad. Why don't *I* drive us down and stay with him for a while, and you could bring May back.' Seth had just learned to drive.

'Great,' Annie said. 'Then I'll drop you off at the hospital on our way out to May's.'

'He's changed a lot, Seth,' Salter said. 'Don't be surprised at what you find.'

'I imagine. He had a stroke, then fell down and cracked his poor old noggin. That would take it out of anybody.' He spoke blithely, flicking away Salter's concern. 'Don't worry. I'm a big boy now.'

'No, I mean, well, physically, yeah, he's shrunk and he's badly bruised, but mentally, I mean. He's hallucinating. He sees people in the room who aren't there, though I think he sees who's really there, too, all mixed up with these ... ghosts. But it's hard to know

how to respond when he suddenly starts talking to
someone at the end of the bed.'

'Don't *worry,* Dad. I'd like to visit my grandfather
in hospital. OK?' He stood up from the table. 'I'll get
my jacket.'

'It's his idea, Charlie. Leave him alone,' Annie said.

While they waited, Salter said, 'This being too much
for you? Me?'

'What? My wanting some time off, you mean? Oh
no. It's May. I don't want to listen to her talking about
him all night again. I've run out of responses.'

'You could go back to work tomorrow.'

'Or the day after. I'll see.'

AT THE HOSPITAL he considered lying to May but in
the end told her that he was going home himself, later,
and he would be back first thing in the morning. He
anticipated some opposition, but his 'take-charge' attitude seemed to relieve her and she waited for him
without any fuss. He left Seth in the room and drove
her home.

When he returned, Seth was still watching. 'I don't
have to be anywhere for another hour,' he said. 'Why
don't you go for a walk?'

SALTER SETTLED HIMSELF in the waiting-room with
his journal. *Saw three more today,* he wrote. *Jennifer
Benson was the other serious candidate, so whatever
they do now, even if they have another election, she
must have a good chance, a possibility that will have
President Jones pissing his pants, and maybe Joan
Dooley hers, too.*

Benson is enjoying herself. She ran against Lyall because no one else would, and she's very sceptical about everyone else's motives. Left-wing, of course, but too cheerful to be a fanatic. Schreiber says she's bitter, but I don't get that impression at all. You have to take things personally to be bitter. She doesn't. I don't think she wants the job at all, and if she gets it she'll last about six months, I should think. She'll do whatever she thinks is right, and have a good time doing it. On paper, she adds up like Schreiber. Both call themselves anarchists; I think they must mean different things by it, though neither one has any illusions about their colleagues or their bosses. What's the difference, then? I'd sooner work for her than for him. No. I would, but that's not the point. Let's just say that she seems like her own woman. All this sounds very flattering, but in the end there's something missing in her, something that would make her useless at getting anything done. She enjoys fighting, but doesn't know what to do with the territory she's won. But she'd look after the troops, and I don't know if Schreiber would.

Next came a guy named Monkman, one of the also-rans with about as much chance of getting the job as I have of becoming chief of police. No hidden depths there. Hidden shallows?

Last, I saw a smooth customer called Prince. Very young, but very dry behind the ears. Only been around for a year but very sure of himself.

Salter read over the page, then put down his pen feeling pleased with himself. He might soon get to the point of having to keep the journal under lock and key. He left the room and walked quietly along the corridor, pausing outside his father's room, hearing his son's voice. He moved closer to the door and listened carefully, ready to help out. Seth was reading aloud. He could now call himself a professional actor, and he was giving his reading voice a workout. The words rolled along, rhythmically, formally: 'The fair breeze blew, the white foam flew, / The furrow followed free; / We were the first that ever burst / Into that silent sea.'

Salter looked carefully round the curtain. Seth was totally caught up in what he was reading. In the crib, the old man lay on his side, his knees curled up, his eyes closed, his mouth slightly open, smiling.

Salter went back to the waiting-room and sat down again.

'The Ancient Mariner.' The only poem his father respected, and from which he could quote, more or less accurately, many stanzas, learned as a project in a Cabbagetown school sixty years before. His father's store of literature.

In the last few days Salter (and May) had tried chatting, television, radio, telling him what was in the newspaper, trying to respond when the old man blurted out a fragment of memory. But it took Seth to know that the way to comfort his father was to read him his favourite poem. Why hadn't Salter known that?

IN THE MORNING, before he returned to the college, he arranged to meet Lyall's cleaning lady at the house. Although there was a statement from her on file, Salter wanted to listen to her talk about Lyall on the principle that no man is a hero to his cleaning lady.

He waited at the kerb, watching for her to walk down the street. He was surprised when a 504 Peugeot pulled up alongside and the window rolled down. 'You policeman?' she called out. 'I park round the back. Meet you there.' She drove down the street, turned around and came back past him and disappeared down the lane. Salter walked to the side of the house where he could watch for her to come in the back gate.

She was perhaps fifty, Portuguese and attractive, with a face that wanted to smile. He shook hands with her, putting on a big smile to show there was no cultural need to look mournful as far as he was concerned, and led her into the house.

'Poor Mr Lyall,' she said as they sat in the kitchen.

This was the first word of regret that Salter had heard so far. 'You liked working for him?' he asked.

'Sure. He never worry if I'm late or not come one week. Nice man. Easy.'

'Did you like him. Himself.'

'Nyah,' she said and wiggled her hand back and forth. 'He was OK. He never try to touch me, like some men who live alone. But he never say much. You know? I was servant. That's OK. He pay for my holidays.'

'Take me round,' Salter said, pretending it was all new to him.

They started on the ground floor. 'Tell me how you found the place when you came in.'

'Everything all over the floor. All the drawers, the cupboards, everything. I put it all back, but no time to clean.'

'Did you get paid?'

'No, I don't want money for that. Why? You pay me?' She laughed to show that her question was a tease.

They moved up to the first floor and then to the second, as she described the condition of the rooms when she arrived.

'You told the police that there was a silver tray missing, and a watch. Was that all?'

'I'm looking, I'm looking. I can't see nothing gone.' Then, moving to Lyall's study, she asked, 'You find the money in the desk?'

This was the money Judy Kurelek had mentioned. 'Cash?'

'Money, yes. He keep a lot of money in the drawer.' She opened it and poked around inside. 'Is gone,' she said, continuing to poke in the drawer. 'Big pile of money. He had a garage sale a month ago and he give me all the stuff no one buy because I help him. After, he put all the money in this drawer. He pay me with it, every week. I tell him I don't like because if someone take it he could blame me. He said not to worry. He trust me. I never touch it.'

'I guess someone found it. Anything else?'

'I don't see nothing.'

Salter said, 'Got time for coffee? There's a good place on Yonge Street.'

'You pay my parking ticket if the man come?' She cackled happily and looked at her watch. 'I go at quarter to two. OK?'

The back room of Le Petit Gourmet was almost empty. Salter got them seated and ordered a slice of quiche for himself and coffee for both of them. As he left the counter, she called, 'I like one of those little cakes, with the chocolate,' and blushed and giggled at her own presumptuousness.

While they were waiting for the microwave to ping, he considered how to get her to talk.

'You find the guy yet?' she asked. She shook her head, answering her own question. 'So many bad people. The other night, last week, two men tried to rob my son outside the house.'

'What happened?'

'I was just coming home. I saw them. I say, you men, stop that. Then Mrs Rogero she come out of the house next door and kick them. We made them run away.'

Salter laughed. 'Did you beat them up badly?'

'Sure. I use my umbrella. Mrs Rogero kick them with her feet.' She laughed. 'Mrs Rogero great big lady. She call them bad words in Portuguese and kick, kick, kick. She wearing her husband's old boots. Outside my house!'

The quiche arrived and Salter found an opening. 'You ever cook for Mr Lyall?'

'Little bit. Not much. I don't like to cook. I clean.'

'Did he have a girlfriend?'

'Sure. Lots. He have one now. Not to sleep over. I never saw her. I think so. Sure. Sometimes I see things. You know. Kleenex, lipstick.'

'Where?'

'Where you think? Upstairs. I think he just bring her home, but not stay all night. That's OK. His wife went away. But I don't know. I don't know why Mr Lyall leave his wife. She was a nice lady. Maybe she not nice to him, eh?'

'When did they separate?'

'Ten years. I clean for her, too. She's a nice lady but too, you know?' She put her hands together in an expression of piety.

'You know what happened?'

'Sure. Mr Lyall go dancey-dancey with other ladies.'

'You have her address?'

'I don't want to make trouble for her.'

'She won't know where I got it. You'll be looking for another job now.'

'I got lotsa work. All my ladies got friends who want me. But you know, in a new place they watch you all the time, make sure you polish right, don't take things. Ahhh!' She threw her hands up in disgust. 'I too old for that.' She picked up her purse. 'Now I got to go.'

He took down her phone number and thanked her.

'You need a cleaning lady?'

'I'll ask my wife.'

'It's OK. I thought maybe you live by yourself. Not so fussy.'

ELEVEN

'CHARLIE,' Marinelli called as he was passing the door. 'Come on in. I've got something for you. You found who was sending the notes, by the way?'

Salter sat down in front of Marinelli's desk. 'I've eliminated one guy,' he said. 'Let me tell you about that place.' He launched into an account of Bathurst faculty and administration, ending with a thumbnail sketch of Fred Leitch, the only person he did not suspect.

Marinelli laughed. 'How's your dad?'

'He's holding his own.'

'I figured he must be. You look a little better yourself. I wanted to tell you, we've got a bite.' He hunched himself forward, full of news. 'Temperance Jewellers on Church Street. Where the hell did a pawnbroker get a name like that? From the street sign? Anyway they reported receiving one Spanish Andalusian Express wristwatch as described in our news release. I've sent a car over to pick it up.'

'When?'

'Last week on Friday.'

'Do they know who they bought it from?'

'They have him on video. They were suspicious, so they activated their theft camera and there he is.'

'What made them suspicious?'

'They wondered why an Indian, a native-type person, would have been spending time in Spain, or alternatively, who would give a panhandler a perfectly good watch. So they guessed it was stolen.'

'And got in touch with us right away?'

'They planned to, they said. Our bulletin reminded them.'

'So where is he?'

'Somewhere downtown. Wandering around. We'll have him by tonight. I guess that's it for you, eh, Charlie?'

'We still don't know who sent the notes, or why.'

'Doesn't matter now, does it? Like you said, some shit-disturber with a light teaching load.'

'You mind if I talk to the pawnbroker?'

Marinelli leaned back. 'We already did. We've got the picture. What's up, Charlie?'

'I'm just curious.'

'You don't look too pleased.' Marinelli laughed. 'You don't want to believe it, do you? You want this to be some clever, academic-type murder, don't you?'

Salter tried not to show what he was feeling. 'I've found seven good suspects. I don't want to waste them. No, I want to find out who wrote those notes.'

'OK, be my guest. But we'll have it wrapped up by tonight.'

Marinelli was right—Salter was disappointed. The Bathurst investigation was just enough of a distraction for him to have hoped to go on with it for a few more days. The Affair of the Dean's Appointment, as he had begun to think of it, would have been fun to get to the bottom of, to find out what all the vote-switching was all about, but if Marinelli had a good suspect, the deputy would not let him waste any more time. The anonymous author would have to find

someone else to send his notes to, and Salter would
have to go back to writing reports.

TEMPERANCE JEWELLERS bought and sold for cash,
but they kept records.

'He was an Indian,' the owner began as he was
looking up the transaction. His mouth was fringed
with hair and he pushed his lips in and out continu-
ously as though getting ready to kiss. It was like talking to a blowfish.

'So I heard. How do you know?'

The owner looked at Salter more carefully. 'OK. He
was the kind of guy we used to mean when we used to
say, "He looks like an Indian." What's the matter,
chief? Did I get the language wrong? I know you're
not supposed to say "Negro" or "Eskimo" these
days, but I thought "Indian" was all right. North
American Indian, I mean, not Hindu or like that.' He
put the tips of his fingers against his lips and gave out
a small war whoop. 'Tonto,' he concluded.

'How do you tell?'

'I don't know. Some deep instinct I have. I could
always tell. What's this all about? He was an Indian,
for Chrissake, like you are white and that guy out
there is Asiatic, who knows which kind? There are lots
of Indians around here.' He went back to searching for
the entry in his ledger.

'When did he come in?'

'Friday morning at nine-thirty. He was sitting on the
step when I opened up. He needed a drink.'

'What did you give him for the watch?'

'I *loaned* him five dollars. My donation to the aboriginal people. The watch is worth a lot more, but I was afraid I wouldn't get to keep it.'

'Did you get his name?'

'Of course. His real name, too.'

'How do you know?'

'Henry Littledeer. You wouldn't make up a name like that, would you?'

'Was he wearing it?'

'The watch? No, he had it wrapped up in a piece of rag inside his shirt.'

'You haven't seen him since?'

'No, but he's got thirty days to redeem it.'

PITY, Salter wrote that night. *It was getting interesting, and I'd still like to know who wrote those notes. Probably Integrity Gerald. Now I'll have to find something else to do while I'm waiting.*

So after all this it turns out to be an Indian named Henry Littledeer. I was hoping I could pin it on the president.

He put down his pencil and went along the corridor. Finding his father asleep, he went back to his tale. For that is what it had become, even in embryo, a tale he was writing while he did his duty by his father.

Refusing to give up hope, he tried to play devil's advocate.

What kind of story are we going to get from him? he wrote. *Probably he'll admit to robbing the house, but he'll say that it was empty when he did. I hope so. That'll keep me going for a couple of days.*

'His prints weren't on the gun, members of the jury.'

'He was obviously wearing gloves.'

'In this weather? No one said anything about rain that night. In all the evidence we heard about the scene of the crime, no one has mentioned mud. I think if we check, we'll find it was a fine dry night. Fireworks Night, if you remember. Thank you, yes. It was not raining. Now, you remember the temperature that night? Ask yourselves, ladies and gentlemen, how many street people, people of any kind, would be wearing gloves in weather like that?'

'He wiped the gun.'

'The defence has already agreed that Mr Littledeer may have been drinking that night, probably was. Now we are being asked to believe that Mr Littledeer, who, we assert, wandered into the house looking for a drink, after killing Mr Lyall, methodically and carefully wiped away the evidence.'

'He had the watch.'

'He found it. Someone gave it to him.'

'Mr Salter, your wife would like to speak to you.' The nurse stood in the doorway.

Salter walked down to the nursing station and picked up the phone. 'I'm coming home, Annie. He's quiet now and—what's the word?—stable. Physically, anyway. He still isn't sure where he is. Yeah. In an hour.'

He went back and added two items to his journal.

1) Get final statements from the college gang.
2) Check the street.

HE DIDN'T CALL in to the office the next morning in case anyone asked him what he was doing.

He found Jennifer Benson between classes and explained what he wanted. 'What we guessed from the start has been pretty much confirmed. It looks as if Lyall was killed by someone robbing him. But a good defence lawyer would look around for other possibilities that we haven't checked. He'd find out what I have, and point out there are a number of people with reasons for disliking Lyall, and they haven't been adequately investigated. See, the evidence against this man is circumstantial. No one saw him do it.'

'What do you want from me?'

'A brief statement about where you were on the night of the 24th and who could verify it.'

'I was at home, reading, and I went to bed early, alone.' She laughed raucously. 'I always sleep by myself on Mondays. My night off. So no one can verify it and I'll come quietly.' She put her wrists out for the handcuffs. 'The truth is, I was with about twenty people at a party in my house. I have a big house in the Annex, and I rent rooms—it's a commune, really, and on May 24 we were having a party. A couple of my tenants are students, and it was sort of their end-of-term. What kind of suspect have you found?'

'We think he's an Indian.'

'A . . . derelict?'

'We haven't found him yet.'

'Poor bastard.'

It was not a cry of anguish. Once more Salter was intrigued by her attitude which seemed cheerful and unsentimental. She had no illusions about some of the people she fought and demonstrated for but their individual failings never made her doubt which side she should be on.

CZERNY-SMITH'S STORY was that after an argument with his wife he had gone for a drive, returning after midnight to an empty house because his wife had gone to stay with friends. She had returned the next day in order to formally move out. He was unable to provide witnesses to his drive, which took up the hours from sunset to midnight. It was such a weak story that Salter was inclined to believe it.

He returned to Gibson Avenue and spent two hours knocking on doors. This job had already been done by Marinelli's detectives, but now Salter had a more specific question. Under the guise of asking if anyone had seen any Indians around on May 24, he was able to establish that no one had seen a stranger of any kind on the night of the murder, male or female, Caucasian, black or aboriginal. One woman believed she had seen an Indian walking along the lane behind the house the next morning. It seemed unlikely to be connected with a killing ten or twelve hours previously, but Salter made a note of it.

It was not conclusive, of course. Many of the owners were at work, their houses and children being taken care of by a variety of Filipino and black nurses and housekeepers. But in this kind of inquiry, there was such a strong desire on the part of those questioned to remember strangers, especially from other classes and cultures, that the absence of any sight at all was persuasive.

MARINELLI SAID, 'We've got him.'

'Who?'

'Littledeer. The Indian who killed the professor.'

'He confess?'

'The guy at Temperance Jewellers made the identification, and Littledeer agrees he hocked the watch.'

'But someone gave it to him.'

'He doesn't even claim that. He can't remember, he says.'

'That's not much to go to court with.'

'It's a piss-poor story, though, and his prints check with some we found in the basement.'

'That'll do it, then, I guess. What is he, a derelict?'

'Why? What the hell's gotten into you, Charlie? The deputy's happy. What's the problem?'

'I've gotten interested.'

'It's black and white.'

'I guess. You mind if I go down to the jail and talk to him?'

'What about?'

'I'd like to hear his story for myself.'

'He doesn't have a story.'

'I'll call in on my way home.'

Marinelli shrugged. 'OK, but if you find anything that should worry me, tell me, won't you. You're supposed to be on our side, remember.'

'Can I have a copy of the report?'

Marinelli called up Littledeer's case on the screen, then pressed the 'print' button. In a few seconds the machine in the corner of the room spilled out the report. Marinelli tore it off and looked in a folder for a photograph, which he clipped to the report and passed across the desk.

The picture showed a familiar face, a face like a hundred others on the street, bruised, scarred, one eye apparently permanently closed, no teeth in the upper jaw and only a few stumps in the lower; black hair hanging to his shoulders and a straggle of hairs posing as a moustache.

'We picked him up last night. The boys say he wasn't in very good shape.'

'What happens now? Legal Aid?'

'We've got a liaison officer for native people in trouble. He's informed the Native Centre. They'll make sure of his rights.'

'You think he robbed the house before he killed Lyall, or after?'

'What am I supposed to do? All the other evidence is there.'

'Maybe he'll tell me. I'll go down and talk to him.'

'Why, for Chrissake? Why?'

'Because I've got some spare time.'

'On one condition. I told you, if you find anything that bothers you, tell me first.'

'Of course.'

'What do you want to do?'

'Talk to him. Read the report.'

TWELVE

SALTER READ THE REPORT through, then, finding nothing he did not already know, drove to the detention centre to get a look at Littledeer.

The Indian had now been in custody long enough to be sober, but otherwise he looked like his picture. He appeared to be about fifty, but Salter judged he could easily be ten years younger, and the victim of many assaults himself.

They sat on either side of the table. The guard stood by the door, not to monitor the conversation, but to be available if needed.

Now that he was here, Salter had very few questions, but he wanted to go over the ground again. First he made it clear that they were not having an official conversation, and that Littledeer did not have to stay if he did not want.

'You a cop?' Littledeer asked.

Salter nodded.

'You the big guy?'

'As far as you're concerned, Henry, I'm nobody, I told you.'

Littledeer shook his head. 'You're the guy in charge.'

'I'm not in charge of anything.'

'Gimme a smoke.'

Salter shook his head and looked at the guard, who produced a cigarette and some matches.

'See?' Littledeer said. 'I bin askin' this guy all day for a smoke. Soon's you come, I get one. That's what I mean.'

'I was up at the house where that teacher lived,' Salter said.

'Oh, yeah?' Littledeer looked away. 'I thought you was just come to make me a social visit.' With each drag he took, about a third of the cigarette disappeared.

'Where did you find the gun?'

'In the house, I guess.'

'Where?'

Littledeer arranged the last quarter-inch of the unfiltered cigarette between his thumb and first two fingers, then put all three digits in his mouth and inhaled deeply, consuming the end of the cigarette and rubbing the glowing cinder that remained to fragments.

'Doesn't that hurt?'

'Not if you wet your fingers. I don't remember where I found the gun. Wherever he kept it, I guess.'

'You were in every room?'

'I guess.'

'You don't remember anything about it?'

'Jesus. The other guys wrote it all down. I woke up on Friday morning in an alley on Church Street. Someone had put the boots to me and I needed a drink. I didn't have no money, but I had this watch, so I hocked it. Later on your guys picked me up.'

'You don't remember where you got the watch?'

'Gimme another smoke.'

The guard looked sour, but under Salter's eye he dropped a handful of cigarettes in front of Littledeer who put them in his shirt-pocket. 'Last thing I re-

member was being in a tavern. Maybe a few days ago.
I bin on a bender.'

'Where did you get the money.'

'I had some money. Sure. Lotsa money. All gone
now.'

'You don't remember where you were on Victoria
Day?'

'Huh?'

'When they let off fireworks.'

'I see fireworks, sure.'

'Where?'

'In the sky.'

'You remember being in the house? Did the guy
have the gun in his room? Did you take it off him?
Was he sleeping?'

'I don't remember.' Littledeer lit another cigarette,
and squinted in his shirt pocket to see how many were
left. 'I had his watch, though, didn't I?'

'The pawnbroker says you did.'

'Uh-huh.'

'Do you remember being with anyone? Were there
two of you?'

'I don't remember.'

'You don't seem very concerned, Henry.'

'I bin in jail before. It's not so bad. They let me
alone. What can you do? Some drunked-up Indian
shot a guy wit' his own gun. It was an accident.'

'That what your lawyer says?'

'Yeah.'

'Wants you to plead guilty?'

'Of an accident. Yeah.'

It was probably the simplest way. Criminal negli-
gence, manslaughter, accidental homicide—Salter did

not know the distinctions without looking them up. The jury would like his name: Henry Littledeer, the pathetic victim of the white man's policies. Which he was, personally and in general. Salter could hear the lawyer's plea already: 'The end product of policies begun by a company of gentleman adventurers in the seventeenth century. First his land stolen, then his lakes and rivers poisoned, his way of life destroyed, and now a neglect that amounts to genocide.' He could have conducted Littledeer's defence himself.

He had spent one summer in the bush in Northern Ontario, first with the Lands and Forests Department, as it was then, as a fire-fighter, then at a tourist lodge on the Lake of the Woods as a labourer, and finally, for three months at the end of that summer and into the fall, at a fishing and hunting lodge fifty miles north of Kenora. His experience at this last job had stayed with him. He had worked with enough Indians long enough to know them as individuals, so that forever afterwards he could summon up a face to give the lie to any attempt at generalizations, whether the generalization was negative, patronizing, or, more lately, romantic. But that the Indian people had been victimized no one could any longer doubt. The lodge north of Kenora where he had worked was closed now because the entire area, including some nearly virgin lakes teeming with fish when he was there, had been poisoned by the mercury used in processing woodpulp; many of the Indian band he had worked with had been reduced to welfare cases with no escape except alcohol.

Salter contemplated asking the guard for the rest of his cigarettes, paying him for them, to give to Littledeer, but he didn't, and the fact that he was not sure if he should have epitomized once more his own unease. Later on, brooding about it, trying to get it straight for his journal, he came to the conclusion that in all the possible understandings and results of the gesture or the failure to make it, the one that would have left him most braced would have been if he had gone through with it and Littledeer had told him to stick the cigarettes up his arse.

Now he said, 'How long have you been on the street, Henry?'

'I'm not on the street. I got a job. I was laid off for a few days. I'm not on the street.'

'Who do you work for?'

'Abe Cooper.'

'Who's he?'

'He's the owner.'

'Of what? What are we talking about, Henry?'

'The Blue Jay company.'

'You work for the Blue Jays? What are you, the pitching coach?' The tall story, he remembered, was a staple of Indian humour in north-west Ontario. It had featured in a lot of the teasing of young white summer workers.

'Not the ball team. The roofing company.'

'When did you work last?'

'Couple weeks. Few weeks. Not so long. Look.' He rolled up his trouser leg and showed a small patch of newly healed skin on his calf. 'Drop of hot tar,' he said.

'OK, Henry,' he said, realizing at the same time that in using Littledeer's first name so often he was being routinely patronizing. He got up. 'I'll be back.'

'Bring me some snooze.'

'Chewing tobacco,' the guard explained.

'I know what snooze is,' Salter told him. 'Copen-hagen?' he asked Littledeer.

Never mind the evidence. It was impossible to fit the crime to Henry Littledeer.

HE CALLED IN TO the hospital on his way back to the office to find his father sitting up in bed, with May in a chair beside him, knitting, ready to be of service.

'You'll be busy,' his father said as soon as he walked in.

Salter waited for the context.

'After a night like that. Sounded like war was de-clared out there. Christ. Guns. Ambulances. Fire-engines. How many were killed?'

May said, 'He's mixed up with the TV.'

The old man looked at her in a considering way. 'That wasn't on television. I'd have switched it off. That was going on out there. And what about out there?' He pointed to the door. 'They don't allow that on television, do they?'

'He thinks he heard the doctors and nurses again . . . enjoying each other . . . in the corridor.'

'Screwing their brains out. And some of the pa-tients. Non-stop. All night. The bloody lot of them. Disgusting.'

'You were dreaming,' May said. 'Fantasizing. Just jealous.'

Salter was impressed at the good instinct May had for what the old man could be told without upsetting him. For his own part he found himself rehearsing every sentence for fear that he would open a window best left closed. It wasn't very different from talking to Henry Littledeer.

'Was I?' his father said. He looked at Salter. 'Let's get out of here. Get Dad. Let's go home.'

'As soon as the doctor says so.'

'One time last night I heard them beating up the other patients. The bell rang before they got to me.'

'It's the drugs,' May said into her knitting. 'The nurse said they had that effect.'

A doctor appeared, accompanied by the ward nurse, and looked at the old man's chart. They ignored Salter and May, so as they were leaving, Salter got ahead of them and stopped them outside.

'How is he?' Salter asked.

The doctor looked queryingly at the nurse.

'I'm his son.'

'He's stable.'

Salter said, 'He seems to me to be raving. Is his brain damaged? What's the forecast? What should I expect?'

'Hasn't anyone talked to you?'

'Not lately. Not so you'd notice.'

The doctor looked at the nurse who shrugged and said, 'I'm just back after a four-day break.'

The doctor took Salter's arm and led him into a recess with two chairs. They sat down and he took the clipboard the nurse was carrying and read through the report. 'Your father had a fall and we checked him for fractures and for a stroke. There seems to be a hair-line fracture but I don't think it's serious—it may even be an old one. There is evidence of a number of small strokes during the past year. Have you noticed him slowing down, maybe stumbling a little when he's tired? There's nothing for us to cure. He needs look-ing after—he doesn't live alone? No, OK—he'll prob-ably recover to about ninety-five per cent of his old self, but he's had a bad shake-up and he's not young.'

'What drug is he on?'

The doctor looked at his chart. 'It's a painkiller. Oh yes, he's getting a tranquillizer, too. Apparently he gets restless in the night.'

'Does he have to have it? I mean, is it essential to his recovery, like—Christ, I don't know—like penicillin or something? Or is it just to keep him quiet?'

'It's a tranquillizer. To make him comfortable.'

'Can you take him off it?'

'It's not advisable.'

'Why?'

'It makes him difficult to nurse.'

'So he's getting it for the nurses' benefit, right? But it's giving him hallucinations. Take him off it.' Salter drew a breath. 'Take him off it. I'll stay with him at night. There's someone here all day.'

'Is that lady your mother?'

'No. She's his common-law wife.'

'Does she agree with you?'

'Yes.'

'All right.' He nodded to the nurse. 'Let's try it. Let me know how he reacts.'

Salter went across the hall and reported to May. 'I'll stay here till you come tonight, then,' she said, and resumed her knitting.

THIRTEEN

THE NEXT MORNING Salter called the owner of the Blue Jay Roofing Company and asked for an estimate on a new roof. A small stain had appeared six months earlier in the corner of the ceiling on the third floor and now would be a good time to have it fixed.

ABEL COOPER, the owner of Blue Jay Roofing, also did rough carpentry, and after Salter had got an estimate for a roof, he picked Cooper's brains about a new fence he needed, and about what a new deck in the back yard might cost. Then he offered him a beer and told him what he really wanted to know.

Cooper knew immediately who Salter was talking about; he had just finished a conversation with Littledeer's legal aid lawyer. He knew Henry, he said, an Ojibway, a good worker when he was sober. Cooper told Salter that he had a high turnover rate among his helpers, partly because the work was unskilled and the pay was poor, partly because Cooper could not guarantee more than a week's employment at a time, and partly, Salter guessed, because working alongside the owner of a small business is always hard work, harder if the business is in construction. Many of them quit on the first day, Cooper said, occasionally by noon. But Henry Littledeer and his brother Billy had been among his best workers, keeping up with Cooper all day and wanting to carry on while the light held. But first Billy, then Henry, fell off the wagon, and stayed drunk until their money ran out and Henry's wife had left him and taken their two children back to Parry Sound, and Henry was reduced to begging and living in one of the shelters for the homeless downtown. It could happen very quickly.

A social worker who had come to see him told Cooper some of Henry's early story in an effort to try and get Cooper to take Henry back, and Cooper had agreed to give the Indian another chance, though he had been badly let down in the middle of a job the last time, but Littledeer had never turned up, and when Cooper checked the shelter which was his only address, he found Henry bruised, cut, and incoherent after an encounter with some winos in an alley the night before. That was the last he had seen of Littledeer until now a legal aid lawyer was asking him to testify to the Indian's good character.

'It isn't difficult,' Salter said. 'All you have to do is stand up and say he worked hard for you and didn't steal anything off you, that you never saw any sign of violence in him. Stuff like that. The lawyer will lead you.'

'The thing is, the last time I saw him he was in a hell of a state. Christ, he was pitiful. He didn't even know me. I don't think he's got any brain left, you know? From drinking shaving lotion and shit like that. But I don't see how he could have broken into a house, search it, find a gun, load it, kill the owner, then get out of there without anyone seeing him. Not in the shape he's been in the last month. They say the house is on Gibson. I've worked on that street. If they even *saw* someone like Henry they'd call the cops right away. He's probably always got *some* blood on him, and he never shaved much.'

Salter said, 'They have the evidence.'

'I don't know what it could be.'

'When he broke into the house, he might have been in better shape than when you saw him. He's been able to stay off the stuff before, you say.'

'If that's the case, then he wouldn't have done it. Henry isn't *bad*, just kinda down the pipe. Indians shouldn't drink; everyone knows that. They've got a gene missing, guy was telling me. But sober, they can be good workers.'

Cooper sounded exactly like the people Salter had known on construction gangs he had worked on thirty years before, with about the same level of benevolent racism as his father, and he saw that Cooper's racism was a reason for taking his concern for Littledeer seriously: in a sense he was talking about the difference between Henry Littledeer and Indians generally, as he understood them.

'So,' Salter said, 'either he was drunk and couldn't have done it, or he was sober and wouldn't have done it.'

'That's about it.'

'You going to testify for him?'

'Somebody has to. Go and see him. He's a totally pathetic human being.'

'The lawyer will probably argue that he's a victim and if there's a reporter and a representative from the Native Council in court, the prosecution will agree and they will get together with the judge to see how to minimize the damage they can do to him, even if he did kill one of their own kind. Everyone feels guilty about everything these days, especially about the Indians. So he'll be handled as gently as possible. But he did kill a professor and you have to lock him up for a while.'

'Would you go and see him?'

'Why?' There was no harm in leaving Cooper with the impression that he had persuaded Salter.

'Somebody ought to.'

'Why?'

'Because I think you guys are full of shit. Henry Littledeer didn't kill anybody.'

'Take it easy. All right, I'll go and see him, and I'll find out what the case is against him.'

'When? Can I call you?'

'No, you can't. I'm not reporting back to you. You've unloaded on me. That's the end of it.'

'That's it?'

'If you don't like it, hire Littledeer a lawyer yourself.'

Cooper nodded eight or ten times to show he was thinking. Then he slapped his knees and stood up. 'OK, Mr Salter. We'll be here to start your roof on Friday.'

THE NEXT MORNING there was a call from Barbara Czerny-Smith, the public relations officer at Bathurst College, asking to see him immediately. He arranged to wait for her in his office. He avoided Marinelli, not wanting to hear that the last conclusive piece of evidence that proved he was wasting his time had appeared.

Barbara Czerny-Smith was so tense she started speaking before she sat down. 'I'm here to express a concern about the man you are holding for the killing of Maurice Lyall,' she said.

Salter moved behind her to close the door and guide her to a chair. He wanted to tell her she had the wrong man, but it was reasonable in view of the time he had spent interviewing the Bathurst faculty to assume he had some status in the affair.

'What's your concern?' he asked.

'This case will be linked with Bathurst College in the public mind. We want to be sure that he is being properly represented.'

'I see. And the accused man is an Indian, and you're worried about the college's image.' He made a mental note to warn Marinelli.

'We are concerned that the good name of the college be preserved.'

'That's two concerns, for you and for him. I can tell you that he already has a lawyer from legal aid. I'll find out who that is, and if you give me a call this afternoon, I'll let you know his name. Or you can get it yourself. Call around. Ask your own lawyer.'

'Thank you.'

It was clear to Salter that she had got the kind of answer she had expected, an unsatisfying one, and that he or Marinelli would be hearing from her again. He said, 'You should know that we have a liaison officer who works with cases like this. If an aboriginal person seems to be concerned with a crime, we let this officer know, he lets the Native Centre know, and we take it from there. The guy isn't abandoned.'

'Thank you,' she said again. She searched for an exit line. 'We will be offering him every support we can.'

'Good.'

As soon as she was gone, Salter went to find Marinelli. The homicide detective became very angry. 'Who's been getting to you?' he demanded. 'I thought all the traffic came straight to here.'

'What are you talking about?'

'I'm talking about every mother's uncle who's been dancing in and out of here trying to get Littledeer out of jail. I'm talking about every hyphenated-rights group in Toronto. Mostly the native rights ones. I'm talking about the universal fucking assumption that when we couldn't find the professor's killer we went out and picked us up an Indian, planted the stuff on him and then beat the shit out of him until he confessed.' Marinelli stopped, his eyes moving rapidly from his desk to Salter and around the room as if he expected an attack from any quarter. 'Do they think we still don't know what "visible minority" means, for Chrissake? Two Vietnamese gunmen shoot up a Chinese café and we aren't supposed to notice what colour they are?'

'Been bad, eh?'

'Bad? Jesus, lucky for us I saw it coming and wrapped this guy up in cotton batten.'

'Saw what coming?'

'I heard the old tom-toms, Charlie. We picked this guy up right after that Winnipeg fuck-up. You heard about that? They damn near brought an Indian guy to trial who had been in their own jail on the night he was supposed to have killed someone. They had a confession from him, but they also had his fingerprints, photo, the lot, to show he was in jail that night. So I was very careful, but the bastards still suspect we are

cooking it up. I'm talking about two Metro council-
lors and a newspaper columnist. They don't want to
be confused with facts. They *know* what we're like.'

'I haven't read anything about all this.'

Marinelli allowed a tiny smile, a tremor of the lip
that almost made it to one nostril. 'For once, you
won't. We've had the media in here and gave them a
little peek at the evidence. Pointed out that a trial's got
to be fair to everyone, including the dead guy, and a
big campaign to discredit the investigation could
backfire. Tell me the story. Who's been talking to
you?'

'The community relations woman at the college.'

Marinelli shrugged.

'And the guy who fixed my roof doesn't think Littledeer is capable of it.'

'You trying to get me going? Who the fuck is the
guy who fixed your roof? Littledeer's father?'

'Littledeer worked for him once, a while ago. He
was a good worker, and Cooper, the roofing contrac-
tor, says he doesn't think Littledeer has got it in him.'

'Even if he was drunk?'

'Cooper didn't seem to think he would be violent,
either way.'

'It's nice that Henry's got such faithful friends. We
call him Henry, Charlie. I agree with your roofer.
Henry is harmless. But one way or another, he robbed
a house on Gibson on the night of Victoria Day and in
the course of robbing it he killed the owner.'

'How do you know? No, I mean, it's none of my
business. If you're busy, tell me, but I'm not busy because I think my father's a little better, but I still don't
want to go back to writing that gambling report.'

Marinelli said, 'I'm glad to hear it. About your dad.'

'So tell me what's happening with the case.'

'We have his fingerprints on the gun cupboard in the basement. What else do we need?' Marinelli watched Salter's face. 'Good enough?' he demanded.

'I guess.'

'You look disappointed. Looks like you're going to have to write that gambling report after all.'

Salter said, 'I'll finish interviewing those people at the college. Then I'll give *you* a report.'

'Did you find many suspects?' Marinelli grinned. 'Seven, was it?'

'Just the usual weak alibis from innocent citizens. I'll tuck it away.' Then a small crack of light appeared as he thought about the case, and he stood up. 'I'll let you have it tomorrow.'

'Any time. The file's right there.'

THE THOUGHT had occurred to Salter that no one had in fact broken into Lyall's house. The killer had let himself in, knowing that Lyall did not lock his doors. How would Littledeer know that? And then he realized that Cooper might not have told him everything and he phoned him and Cooper agreed immediately that yes, he had forgotten, but he had in fact worked on Lyall's roof, and Littledeer was helping him at the time. 'I do a lot of work in the area,' Cooper said. 'I must have done three roofs on Gibson.'

'So why didn't you tell me?'

'I reckon it slipped my mind. I wasn't withholding anything.'

There was nothing else to do but hand the detail over to Marinelli, who said, 'That just about does it.'

'Anything else turn up?'

'We've been around the taverns and we've picked up a story that he had a hell of a roll of money on him. Where else could he have got it? When he picked him up he'd been worked over. Why? For a roll of money someone saw?'

'When do you move?'

'We can put it off forever, but why wait?'

'Has his lawyer bought your evidence?'

'Yea. We'll agree before we go into court. I imagine he'll claim booze.' Marinelli looked at his computer screen. 'Foetal alcohol syndrome. He's been affected since birth and he blacks out a lot. Now, for Christ's sake, Charlie, Staff Inspector, sir, leave it alone.'

FOURTEEN

BUT WHEN Barbara Czerny-Smith called that afternoon, it was not to learn about Littledeer, but to inform Salter that she had organized a group of students to help with the investigation.

'You've done what?' Salter put the phone on his desk, jumped up and closed his door. 'To help in what?' he asked, when he sat down.

She repeated. 'I've organized a group of aboriginal students to assist you. We're meeting in my office at three.'

'I'll be right there. Don't do anything else until I get there.' He grabbed his coat and made for the parking lot, hoping to be in time to squelch this initiative before Marinelli heard of it.

'I HAVE ENLISTED the help of the Aboriginal Students' Society,' Czerny-Smith said in her office, twenty minutes later. There was a quacking quality about her voice, and an officiousness about the way her head turned from side to side, which put Salter as much on edge as if she were an entire public committee of busybodies, added to which he felt that in some sense he had created her.

'What is the Aboriginal Students' Society?' he asked. He had a vision of hundreds of Inuit and Indians packing a lecture hall and getting their orders to scour the city for, who was that guy, Peter Lorre? 'M'?

'You'll see. They'll be here soon.'

'I don't want to get too excited while we're waiting. How many are there?'

'Two this year. Sometimes more. We have had as many as five.'

'What are they all about?'

'They are a supportive group. They are going to help us find . . . they're going to advise us.'

'About what?'

'Here's the first now.'

A short fat boy with a straggling moustache came through the door and looked at them warily.

'Come in, come in.' She ran round her desk and placed a chair for the boy.

They sat in silence while Czerny-Smith smiled at the boy, then she said, 'We're just waiting for your friend.'

'My who?'

'Mary Thompson. The—er girl in Early Childhood Education.'

'She's my friend?' The boy looked at Salter to see if he would make sense of this.

'My name's Salter. I'm a policeman.'

'Uh-huh.'

'And yours?'

'My name?' He looked from Salter to Czerny-Smith. 'You asked me to come here. Don't you know who I am?'

'Of course. You must be Matthew Chocolate. Matthew is from Yellowknife. He's in Radio Technology. Isn't that right, Matthew? How long have you been here?' She beamed at him.

Chocolate had trouble keeping his face straight. He turned to Salter, almost grinning. 'I just came down in September for the course. Now I want to go home. The ice just broke up.'

'Why don't you? The courses are over, aren't they?'

'I failed a coupla subjects. I don't want to get behind, spend any more time here than I have to. I'll be home in August for good. What's up? Looks like my friend ain't coming.'

'I'll try and track her down. Let's go ahead.' She cleared her throat and avoided looking at Salter. 'You may have heard, Matthew, that the police are holding a man, a . . . native person, Henry Littledeer.' She explained that on behalf of the college she had an interest in the case.

'The guy they say killed the teacher here?'

'The man who's accused, yes. The college would like to help him. I'm asking you to help me.'

'Do what?'

'First of all, go and see him in prison. He needs visitors.'

'I already failed two courses.'

'Just once or twice. Do you know any other . . . native people . . . in Toronto?'

He looked at her, frowning. 'I live in a hostel full of Indians.'

'Do the other Indians in Toronto know each other?'

'Do the Chinese?'

'Well, there are so many more of them.'

'There's plenty of Indians, too. Sixty thousand of us, last I heard. Toronto's the biggest reservation in Canada. Of *course* we don't all know each other. I know the guys in my hostel, some down at the centre, and the guys on my hockey team. That's about it.'

'Do you ever go to native functions?'

'We play hockey Sunday nights. Otherwise we do our homework and watch television. I don't know about any native functions. Where would they be? *What* would they be? You mean those potlatch suppers at the Centre? I only go to them when there's venison.'

She started again. 'This man we're concerned about, Henry Littledeer, can't remember where he was after Mr Lyall's death until Friday morning.' She turned to Salter. 'I've been talking to Mr Littledeer's lawyer. All the evidence is circumstantial. The police have no eye-witnesses. It's quite possible this evidence was planted.' She looked challengingly at Salter. 'Perhaps *we* could find a witness to testify that he saw Mr Littledeer miles from the scene when he was supposed to be committing the crime?'

'Make sure he's reliable,' Salter said. 'Don't plant one.'

Chocolate said, 'He was probably holed up somewhere, drinking. It's a big problem among us.' He looked at her, then at Salter, then back at Czerny-Smith. 'Ask your friend here,' he said to her.

'What I'm wondering is whether someone might have seen him.'

'Not me.'

'No, I was wondering if you could sort of ask people.'

'Where?'

'I thought you might know the areas he would most likely be in.'

'In Yellowknife I would know. Not here.'

'Do you think you could find out?'

'Mean to get your way, don't you, like my grand-mother? Where's the jail? I told you, I don't go down to those parts of the city. OK, I'll go see him. But look, lady, he might just tell me to... screw off, you know?'

'Then you will have done your best. We will. But he might just give you an idea, don't you think?'

'About what?'

Challenged, she had nowhere to go. 'Anything.'

Chocolate looked at Salter for help.

'Take him some cigarettes,' Salter said.

Chocolate looked back at Czerny-Smith. 'What'll I say?' he demanded. Then his face crinkled. 'I'll tell him the Aboriginal Students' Society is on the war-path. I'll need some money,' he added.

'Here,' she said. 'Here's twenty dollars. Take cabs. It's a very rough area.'

Salter said, 'It's OK if there's three or four of you. People actually live there. My father, for one.'

She blushed. 'I thought it wasn't safe. I don't know it very well.'

Salter ignored her. 'Stay loose, Matthew. Keep your back to the wall.'

'I'll call you,' Chocolate said to Czerny-Smith.

'Can you come by and let us know what you find out tomorrow morning?' Czerny-Smith asked.

'Sure. What time?'

'Ten?'

WHEN SALTER ARRIVED the next morning he bumped into her on the steps of the building. Matthew Chocolate was waiting outside her door. She let them in, and bustled about making coffee.

'How did you find him?' Salter asked while they were waiting.

'That's a helluva place to spend time in.'

'The jail?'

Chocolate nodded and breathed in sharply. 'Good place to stay away from.' He smiled. 'Hey, you know what the guard said? He said, you guys speak English now. No Indian talk.'

'I think that's preposterous,' Czerny-Smith said. 'Suppose you were French Indians!' She turned on Salter but he put his hand up against her voice. 'I don't run the jails. There's a ministry for that.'

But she was not to be denied. 'The idea of incarcerating a possibly innocent man and then not allowing him to use his own language is incredible.'

'He could've been joking,' said Salter, who had caught Chocolate's eye.

'He was. He wasn't comin' on heavy. He was tryin' to make us feel easy.'

'Well, it was in very bad taste. You should have talked in . . . your own language to make the point.'

'Henry's an Ojibway,' Chocolate said. 'I'm Dogrib. We don't talk the same language.'

Salter cut in, feeling sorry for her. 'So how was he?'

'Still drying out. He must have been on a helluva drunk.'

'Did he tell you anything?'

'He can't remember where he was for three days. We talked about a lot of stuff and I think he knew I was on his side, but he just can't remember. He's in bad shape. But I was thinking, if he robbed the house, killed the guy, he must've had someone with him. He wouldn't have made it on his own, 'less the guy was in a wheelchair. What was he doing up there? How come he picked that house? How'd he get in without the guy hearing? There must have been more than just Henry.'

Salter said, 'We've got some good answers, Matthew.'

'Such as?' Czerny-Smith interjected.

Salter ignored her.

'Do you think he has any friends in the area?' she asked Chocolate.

'Near the jail?'

'No, where he usually goes. Near the men's shelter. Queen and Sherbourne,' she ended, triumphant at remembering the corner where the homeless gather.

Chocolate squinted sideways at Salter. 'We're gonna try and find out. Maybe find the other guy.'

She looked at him, excited. 'Who's "we"?'

'Coupla guys at the hostel. They're studying to be carpenters at another college. They're from a reserve up near Timmins. Henry told me where he usually hangs out, so we figured we'd go down there, see if we can find anyone who knows him.'

Salter cut in sharply. 'You even get a hint that there's another guy around, you get right back to me. Leave it alone then, OK?'

'Surely the police would have done that when they were looking for him in the first place.'

Salter looked away.

Chocolate said, 'We figure no one would have talked to the cops, or said they was with him. But they might tell us. These guys at the hostel think it's worth a try.'

'It helps to speak the language,' she said, looking at Salter in triumph.

'I told you, I speak Dogrib; these two guys are Ontario Indians, like Henry. They speak Ojibway, too. We talk English to each other, just like white men. Yeah, I'll need a few more bucks, too. For expenses. To buy guys a beer.' He grinned at Salter.

Now she looked hesitantly to the policeman for guidance.

Salter gave him twenty dollars. 'And here's a picture of Littledeer,' he added.

When Chocolate had gone, he said, 'I'll tell Inspector Marinelli. He won't like it, though.'

MARINELLI SAID, 'What's this?' He adopted a newscaster voice and posture. '"An army of amateur helpers fanned out across the city, determined to do what the police had been unable to."' In his normal voice, he added, 'Give me a break, Charlie.'

'There's only three of them, three kids. I told the leader you wouldn't care. By the way, one of them figures that if Littledeer did do it he might have had a partner.' Salter left it there.

Marinelli said, 'And you wondered if maybe there might not be something in it? And if I'd thought of it? We talked about that, remember? Question number nineteen in the opening round of questions. "Who else was there?" you ask. "Tell us and we'll go easy on you." You should watch more television. You know what he said?'

Salter nodded. ' "I can't remember." But it would answer something that's been bothering me, something this kid spoke of in a general way. When I looked the house over, saw the pictures and read the report, it looked like Littledeer had been in every room, opened every drawer in the house. But Lyall was shot in the bedroom on the second floor. So presuming it's Littledeer, did he search the house first, then go into the bedroom with a shotgun he'd found in the basement? It doesn't make sense. Lyall must have surprised him in the bedroom after Lyall got the gun. So when did Littledeer trash the third floor? What kind of thief would hang around poking in the rest of the drawers after he'd killed the owner? From what I've seen, not Littledeer. He'd have run for it. But if there were two of them, one could have searched while the other kept Lyall covered. Then he shot Lyall. Maybe Lyall tried to jump him, maybe they shot him so he wouldn't be able to identify anyone. But it doesn't look as if there was any kind of struggle.'

Marinelli waited in case Salter had the solution. When nothing came, he asked, 'How's your dad?'

'He seems to be turning around. He also seems a lot older. He's tough, but he's weak now, and he's lost some depth perception. He's not sure how far to reach out for things.'

'Keep your fingers crossed,' Marinelli said, meaning nothing.

Salter stood by the door. 'Keep me in touch, eh?'

Marinelli said, 'Those kids are much more likely to report to you than to me. Who is this woman? What's driving her?'

'She seems to think that the college has a duty to Littledeer. I think she began by making sure he had a lawyer.'

'She sounds to me like she's more concerned about poor Indians than dead deans. Stay close to her, will you, Charlie? I don't need a bunch of aboriginals picketing the trial.'

FIFTEEN

TWO DAYS LATER Salter was in Barbara Czerny-Smith's office listening to three Indian boys tell their story. 'We got him sighted all the way back to Tuesday morning,' Matthew Chocolate said. 'That right, Ivan?'

Ivan, a thin solemn boy with spiky hair, said, 'We know where he was from noon on Tuesday to Wednesday night.'

'Where?'

'He was drinking. First in a few taverns around Sherbourne and Queen, then on Wednesday around the liquor store on Front Street next to the market, some of the time in the Market washroom and then in a construction shack behind one of the stores. The cops moved them on both times.'

'Didn't the police report it?' Czerny-Smith asked.

'What's to report?' Salter asked her.

'But when you knew you were looking for an Indian?'

'We didn't know we were looking for an Indian until Friday when Henry turned up at the jeweller's. You mean one of the cops should have reported a drunk around the market? If we did that every time, we'd need two notebooks. Go down to the market on Saturday morning. Anyway, we don't discriminate among drunks—white, black, Indian, Oriental—they're all the same to us.'

The third boy parted the shiny black hair that hung down over the sides of his face, pulled the curtain wide open with his fingers, looked at Salter, smiled, turned to the others and said, 'He's bullshittin' us.'

I may not be the only one, thought Salter. He remembered overhearing an Indian in a grocery store in Kenora, on being told by the manager that there was a special on chicken parts, replying, with a look of wonder, 'But I don't have any chickens need fixing'.

'What are the details?' he asked.

Chocolate nodded to the boy with spiky hair. 'You found them, Ivan.'

Ivan cleared his throat. 'He was most of the time with two others, city Indians. The three of them bought liquor on Wednesday morning down on Front Street, and Henry tried to buy some again in the afternoon, but they wouldn't serve him.'

'Too drunk?'

Ivan nodded.

The boy with the curtain of hair said, 'Assholes.'

Czerny-Smith turned to him interestedly. The rest waited. He shook his hair back off his face. 'If you can't get liquor you don't go home and drink milk.' His voice was rising, incredulous. 'You drink shaving lotion, rubbing alcohol, Chinese cooking wine, any shit you can find. If you can't buy the good stuff you buy the bad stuff and it kills you.'

'Is that what they did?'

Ivan came in. 'No. Henry had plenty of money so he could pay someone to buy for him. That's what they said.'

'What do you think they meant by "plenty"?'

'A wad, they said.'

'Where was he Tuesday morning?'

Chocolate said, 'We couldn't find anyone who saw him until around noon on Tuesday. At that point he was in the Dover Tavern with another guy. Henry was buying for both of them.'

'You know who the other one was?'

'An Indian. He spent the night in the mission, then he was bumming his way along Jarvis, trying to put together the price of a beer when he saw Henry. He knew him; they'd drunk together before, and Henry took him in to the Dover and bought them a few beers. Henry got pretty drunk and the bartender threw them out and this guy lost Henry then. So, Tuesday night Henry disappears but we pick him up on Wednesday morning with the other two. We couldn't find any sign of him on Wednesday night, and then Friday he tried to hock the watch.'

'He said he woke up in an alley. You think those two rolled him?'

Ivan shook his head. 'Someone did, not them. They said they went back to the liquor store by the market on Thursday to see if he was still around, but they couldn't find him. I think they were telling the truth.'

'What were they? Two men?' Salter asked.

'A man and a woman.'

'Indian?'

'Yeah.'

'Would they talk to me?'

'Not if they saw you coming. I don't have no names for you.'

'What about the waiter in the pub? He remember him?'

'He wouldn't talk to me.'

Czerny-Smith said, 'Didn't he know about the Indian charged with murder?'

'If he did, that's why he wouldn't talk to me.'

'OK.' Salter stood up. 'Whereabouts is this pub?'

'Below Dundas.' Chocolate cleared his throat and glanced at the other two. He pulled a piece of paper from the pocket of his windbreaker. 'We had some expenses. Two mickeys of rye, and two submarines for them. Three hamburgers and Cokes for us.'

'How much altogether?'

'Thirty-eight seventy.'

Salter handed over two twenties.

'And our fares,' Ivan said. Matthew laughed.

Salter added another ten, feeling very slightly that he was being conned, but it was worth it. 'Thanks,' he said. 'No sign of anyone else with Henry before he picked up this pal on Jarvis Street?'

'Uh-uh. You want us to try some more and find out where he was Tuesday morning, and Wednesday night? Maybe even Monday night? For a small extra fee?' He grinned at his two mates.

'If I need any more help I'll get hold of you through Mrs Czerny-Smith.'

'Any time.' Chocolate looked at his pals for confirmation of what he was about to say. 'This is *interesting*,' he said.

'Yeah,' Ivan said.

'Real shit,' said the third boy.

HE CALLED in to the hospital to find his father was back in intensive care. He had woken in the night and managed to fight his way off the bed and fall on the floor. Salter glanced briefly at the bed; the old man seemed hardly alive.

'He looks bad,' the nurse said. 'But all the signs are good.'

'What happened?'

'I think he woke up frightened. He's been restless since we took him off the tranquillizer.'

So it's my fault, I guess, thought Salter. 'He's stable, is he?' He was wretched with anger but not with the nurse. With God, perhaps.

Outside in the corridor he tried to comfort May. As soon as he touched her she started to cry and he held on to her for a while until she was calmer, then he set her down on the bench and called Annie, who promised to come down immediately. He could think of no way to alleviate May's misery, so to avoid it he went to get her a paper cup of tea from the store across the street, taking his time about it. When he got back, Annie had arrived. She relieved him of the tea and waved him away. 'I'll look after her,' she said. 'Go to work.'

THE DOVER TAVERN was left over from an older era when men gathered in parlours around Formica tables covered in ten-cent glasses of beer and spent the evening shouting at each other. When Salter walked in, about two o'clock in the afternoon, the noise was nothing like it would be eight hours later but it still made Salter want to fire a shot into the ceiling to gain someone's attention. He found the waiter and identified himself. The waiter looked murderous. 'That fucking kid was in here bothering me. Told me he was looking for his dad,' he said, explosively. 'You got Indians working for you now?'

'He was helping the police with their inquiries. Like you're going to do.'

The waiter stepped back from the look on Salter's face. 'So. What do you want from me? OK, I think he was in here with another Indian one morning. I don't know which day, though.'

'What did he look like?'

'Just the way he did in the picture. I'd seen him before.'

'Was he drunk?'

'Not when he came in. I wouldn't've served him, would I?'

'I'll try that again. Had he been drinking when he came in? I don't want a run-down on the beer-slinger's guide to serving drunks.'

'I'm telling you. No. He was stone cold sober.'

'Was he dirty? Did he look as if he'd slept outside?'

'Sure. Don't they always, those Indians? He looked as if he'd been in a fight, too.'

'How so? Cuts? Bruises? Blood?'

'Nah, not that day, but he had a big plaster on the side of his head.'

'Where? Show me? How big?'

'The size of my hand.' The waiter cupped his hand over his temple. 'Like that.'

'How old was it? The plaster.'

'How the hell should I know? What'll it be, chief?' he called, moving down the counter to a customer.

Salter leaned over and caught his sleeve with two fingers, with the same effect as if he had both hands

on the neck of the man's shirt. 'You've got two hook-
ers sitting over there waiting for customers. Want me
to send the morality squad down? Was the plaster
clean?'

'Yeah.'

'Very clean? Show up in the dark, would it?'

'Pretty clean.'

'Could he have slept on it?'

'It looked like it was new that morning.'

'And they stayed, him and his pal, until you kicked
them out.'

'Yeah, his pal looked about ready to throw up.'

'Did you notice his money?'

'No. He didn't mean you to. He kept sneaking five-
dollar bills out of an inside pocket. Looked like he had
quite a little stack in there.'

'He paid for all the beer?'

'That's how I remember it.'

'And when he left, did you tell anyone else how
much money he seemed to have?'

'Don't try that shit.' He jerked his sleeve out of
Salter's fingers. 'If he got rolled, it was his pal who did
it.'

Salter nodded. 'Probably. Right after he threw up.'

NOW HE HAD a tiny piece of identification. Not all Indians look alike. One of them had a patch on his
forehead.

He started with his own people, the men on the beat
in the division which has the responsibility for downtown Toronto. There were no reports of drunken,
patched-up Indians being picked up on the night of
May 24, nor could anyone remember one.

'Try the street patrol,' the inspector on duty said.

'Who are they?'

'They operate out of the Anishnawbe Health Centre—the Native Affairs place. They man a patrol at night to try and catch any street people who need help. They worry more in the winter, keep them from freezing to death on the streets, distributing food and blankets and stuff. But even now, this rain makes it hard for the people outside.'

'Where are they? This patrol.'

'They work out of a building near the shelter, on Queen Street.'

The man who ran the patrol was away, but Salter found two of the drivers in an upstairs room drinking coffee. One of the men pulled some yellow sheets from a drawer and flipped through them to the report of the night in question. 'Eleven,' he said. 'Three natives.'

'You pick up... the others, too?'

The driver said, 'We're here to help. About two-thirds of the people we find are white.' He turned to the other driver. 'You were on patrol that night, Thomas. See anyone like that?'

'Lots. But I didn't notice anyone with a bandage. You say it was fresh?'

'That's what I heard.'

He bent down to speak through a hatch into the next room. 'You listenin', Betty?'

'I hear you.'

'Did we patch anyone up that night?'

'Not that I remember. Did you try the hospitals?'

And then, while he listened to them speculating about how they might help him, a memory came back, a memory of a man who rolled his truck into the ditch

while he was driving with his knees, a man who had
been detained all night while they shined a light into
his eyes every hour.

Salter said, 'If an ambulance picks up a guy off the
street around here, where would they take him? If they
were answering a 911 call, I mean?'

'Could be any one of them. St Mike's is the nearest
but it might be full that night.'

'Then they have to look for another hospital that
has space, right?'

'Hang on.' The other driver had been dialling a
number as they talked. 'I'm just speaking to the ambulance service.' He listened for a few moments, then
said, 'Thanks,' and put down the phone. 'I thought
so. They operate a Central Resources Registry. All the
hospitals call in and the drivers know all the time
which ones might have space. So it could be any of
them.' He looked triumphant.

'Call them back. No, I will. What's the number?'
He took the telephone from the driver.

The man staffing the communications desk of the
ambulance service said, 'Of course we keep a record.
What's his name? No. No one of that name recorded
that night. Hold on. Indian? Here he is. Picked up in
a lane behind Sam the Record Man on Yonge. No
identification. Probably been rolled. Semi-conscious.
Cut on the head. Took him to Mount Sinai.'

At Mount Sinai, Salter's luck held. The intern who
had been on duty on Monday night was available. He
remembered Henry Littledeer. 'He said he'd been hit
by a door. He had a big contusion on his temple and a
major cut. He tested out all right, except that he
couldn't remember where he got the injury and he was

pretty confused. It took us a long time to get a name out of him. First he said he was Joe Starling or some such name, then he switched to Littledeer, so I kept him in Emergency overnight because of the possibility of concussion.'

'You're sure that was the name?'

'Once he switched to Littledeer, he said it, every hour, all night, when we woke him up. Memorable, isn't it?'

'You're certain he was here all night?'

Even if he slipped out for a few minutes, he was in no state to get very far, but I'll check it.' He went to a desk and played with a computer, then caught sight of a nurse coming through the door. 'Debbie, you were on duty the night that Indian came in, Littledeer, suspected concussion. Remember? Can you confirm he was here all night?'

'I checked him every hour. So did you.'

'This him?' Salter showed them the picture. He did not want to learn later that Henry Littledeer was, in fact, the man who Henry had had the fight with, Joe Starling or some such, who had given Littledeer's name instead of his own. He was too close to the end to risk anything like that.

'That's him.'

'What time did he go?'

'Seven o'clock. We gave him some breakfast and he went on his way.'

SIXTEEN

MARINELLI WAS ANGRY at first, then resigned. 'OK, he didn't do it, I guess. Now explain the fingerprints and the watch.'

'We might have to wait for Littledeer to get some memory back. First he was pissed, probably, then concussed. I'm going to try a couple of things.'

Marinelli said, 'I suppose I ought to be grateful. I mean, better you than his lawyer, or some Indian war party, and better sooner than later. We haven't actually charged him yet, thank Christ. Now find me a new suspect. You didn't find the guy who was with him yet?'

'I'll see what I can do.'

'What?'

'I'll ask Mackenzie if I can stay with it.'

'Don't you have anything else to do?'

'What I have to do requires peace of mind, which I'm short of right now.'

'I thought he was back home?'

'He tried to get out of bed yesterday and had a fall. Hit his head on the floor. They've plugged him in to all their fucking machines again, brain-scanned him and found nothing more except a little bump on his head where he fell over, and now he's full of drugs again and he has to stay there until he's clean and all the new doctors are sure I can't sue them for malpractice. And then what? Maybe it's not fair to let his wife cope with him, even though she's determined to, so I'm wondering if I should be looking for a home. I don't know where to start. My first wife used to work at City Hall. She would have known, but she's gone.'

'The Yellow Pages?'

'For an old folks' home?' Salter picked up the Yellow Pages and flipped through it. 'You're right. There's dozens of them. Thanks. This'll give me something to do, but I'll still follow this up, if you don't mind.'

'Just to take your mind off him?'

'No. I'd like to see what connection Littledeer has with the case. We know he couldn't have killed Lyall, but where did he get the watch?'

'You feel sorry for him?'

'Joe, all you've got on him is unlawful possession. I'll see he doesn't get lost, but I'd like to take him for a drive.'

'Where?'

'To some places he might remember.'

Marinelli leaned back in his chair. 'Sorry for him,' he repeated. 'That's against regulations. You sure you're not just upset over your dad? You must be pretty tired.'

Salter leaned over the desk. 'I'll tell you what it is, Joe. Once, one of our kids, the youngest one, got very ill before he was a year old. There was a good chance he would be crippled for life. He wasn't, because we were very lucky and Annie was quick. See, our paediatrician was pretty young and conscientious, still young enough to look for the worst and most interesting diseases, and he found one in Seth, influenza of the hip or some such, and caught it in time. Twelve

hours more would have been too late. Anyway, for a
week Seth was in hospital hooked up to all the tubes,
and very miserable, and Annie sat by his crib, and then
when she came home she scrubbed the house from top
to bottom, and cooked and gardened and all that, because she thought maybe it was her fault, even though
she was the one who noticed Seth was in pain every
time she put him down and did something about it. I
would have waited a couple of days myself, given him
an aspirin. So though she doesn't believe in God she
thought if there is a God then maybe He would for-
give her if she showed how—what?—penitent?—she
was, and He did. Now I've just got Henry off a homicide charge, right? Maybe my old man will be all
right. Now I'd like to give you a hand.'

'I think you should take a few days off.'

'That's the last thing I want.'

'I'll tell the deputy.'

SALTER SAID, 'I found out where you were on Monday night when the teacher was killed. They're drop-
ping the charges.'

'I can go?' Littledeer looked bemused.

'They've still got you on unlawful possession. The
watch and the money.'

'What money?'

'You were seen to have a lot of money on Tuesday
and Wednesday.'

'Who by?'

'Several people.'

'I must have saved it up.'

'And the watch?'

'Somebody must have give it to me.'

'I wonder about that. I want you to come for a ride with me.'

'Where?'

'Here and there. Try and jog your memory.'

'Do I have to?'

'You could stay here.'

'You gotta smoke?'

Salter produced the cigarettes he had armed himself with. Littledeer started to take a handful.

'You can take the pack.'

Littledeer stashed the packet away and lit up, considering his choices. 'OK. What the fuck. Beats sittin' here with the white men.'

They collected his shoelaces and belt, and a few minutes later they were driving down Jarvis to Front Street. Salter told Littledeer what he knew. 'On Wednesday you bought liquor here. You were with a man and a woman. Indians.'

'Coulda bin Hungry Mary.' Littledeer shook his head. 'You could tell me anything.'

Salter turned the car around and drove up to the Dover Tavern. 'Let's have a beer,' he said.

Littledeer grinned. 'You payin'?'

'Just for one.'

Littledeer drank the beer carefully, treating it like the medicine it was. Salter got a flash of hope when the Indian's gaze rested on the right waiter. 'Sonofabitch,' Littledeer said.

'You know him?'

'He's threw me out of here, two or t'ree times. He don't like Indians.'

'He threw you out on Tuesday night. You had a pal who looked sick.'

'I don't remember.'

They drove across the city to Mount Sinai hospital, parking behind at the Emergency Department. 'You came out of here on Tuesday morning.'

Littledeer shook his head. 'Uh-uh. I came out the other end, on to the main drag.'

'You remember?'

'Drive around to the front.'

Outside the hospital Littledeer looked up and down University Avenue, and said, 'I took the subway. They give me a token to get to the mission but I went the other way.' He grinned. 'This is like one of those movies where you get a dog to pick up a trail, right? I'm the dog *and* the trail.'

'Where did you get off the subway?'

'I don't remember.'

'Why did you get on it?'

'To go to work. That's it. With the roofing guy. I bummed a quarter and called him up, but the crew had gone out already so I went uptown to look for him. He had a couple of jobs around St Clair, I remember. St Clair. That's where I got off the subway. Then I walked south looking for the truck. Yeah. Then I bummed some change for a coffee and a donut and ate them in the cemetery.'

'Then what?'

'Then I musta walked around looking for the roofing guy.'

'Let's take a look.'

Salter started at St Clair, then worked his way south, backwards and forwards between Avenue Road and Yonge Street. Half way along Gibson, Littledeer grabbed his arm. 'There,' he said, pointing to the walkway between houses that led to the park behind. 'I'm pretty sure I went down there.'

Salter pulled the car up on the kerb and they walked through to the lane behind. Littledeer moved ahead and led him to a spot under a tree. 'Here,' he said. Salter bent down and saw the hole under the tangle of huge roots. He brushed the leaves aside, reached in and pulled out a newish-looking yellow leather brief-case. Inside were an antique silver tray and a Mont Blanc pen.

'I was going to come back for them,' Littledeer said.

'Where did you find them?'

'Right there. I saw the yellow when I went to sit down. I was feeling sick again.'

Now Littledeer walked along the path, leading Salter, and stopped outside the back of Lyall's house. 'We fixed his roof,' he said.

'Ever go inside?'

'For a leak. He's got a john in the basement we used.'

'That's the house of the guy who was killed.'

Littledeer nodded. 'I figured that out as I was showing it to you. Good thing you found I was in hospital. Hey, I wasn't in a fight, I walked into a door. I remember. Somebody let one of those big doors swing on me. Then I musta got rolled. I still don't re-member the hospital too well, but I remember com-ing up here and finding the money and stuff, then going down to where I hang out and finding Andy Mackenzie. That's who you found, right?'

'He wouldn't say who he was.'

'Fucking Andy,' Littledeer said warmly. 'I don't remember nothing until you guys picked me up.'

'Who's Joe Starling?'

'Just a guy I know.'

'First you were concussed, then after a night in hospital, you came up here and found the money, then you got drunk for two days, so you were probably concussed *and* pissed.'

'I guess.'

'Let's take a look in the basement.'

He led the Indian through the back door down the steps. 'Where's the washroom?' he asked Littledeer.

The Indian led the way to the back of the basement, pausing by the gun cupboard. 'The lock's gone,' he said.

'Did you try and open it when you worked here?'

'I just saw it was locked. That where he kept his gun?'

'That's what we think.'

Henry nodded. 'I figured.' He pointed to a drawer below the bench. 'He kept the shells in there.'

'What else did you find?'

'I didn't take them. I was just looking around.'

But it made sense. Henry was no angel, and given free run of the basement he probably looked around for something small and valuable to steal, getting curious about a locked cupboard. His fingerprints would be all over it.

'Let's get back. I'm sorry, Henry, but you've still got a couple of charges to face.'

'Sixty days, maybe? Three months?'

'You got a record?'

'Only for fighting; and drunk and stuff. Nothing serious.'

'But lots.'

'Yeah.'

As Salter handed him over at the jail, Littledeer said, 'Maybe you could get them to hurry it up. There's better jails than this.'

'I'll find out how it works. I can't promise.'

THE NEXT MORNING Salter and Marinelli spoke first to the deputy. Salter said, 'There is still the possibility that someone like Henry Littledeer did it, a casual robber, but it's starting to look like a cover-up. Somebody killed Lyall, accidentally or on purpose, and then tried to make it look like a break-and-enter.'

'Why?'

'They stashed the briefcase with the money and a couple of trinkets. Who would do a thing like that? The money was untraceable and fitted nicely into a pocket, as Littledeer found. And Lyall was shot in his bedroom but the whole house was turned over. It's hard to figure a chain of events that works. Possible, but hard. So it's more likely that someone killed Lyall and tried to make it look like a robbery.'

'You want to stay with it?' the deputy asked.

'I'd like to.' He looked at Marinelli. 'I've done a lot of the groundwork already. And I'd like to know, if it was someone on campus, whether they would have let Littledeer take the rap.'

The deputy looked at him. 'This is not a quest, Salter. Just find the killer.' He looked across at Marinelli. 'I know you've got a slate full, Joe. Can you use the help?'

Marinelli nodded, reluctantly, it seemed to Salter.

The deputy turned back to Salter. 'It's a bit of fancy theorizing you're into here. I believe you that this Indian didn't do it, but keep him in mind. Maybe one of his pals did, someone like that. Start knocking on doors, find out who was around. I know, we've done that, but this Indian surfaced pretty quick. You have to do it again. What night was it? Victoria Day? Everybody was outside watching fireworks. Did they have a bonfire on the street? Did you talk to them? What did they all do afterwards? What did you use to do after the fireworks, Joe? Get together with a neighbour for a couple of drinks? These people do that? Where? Whose house? See what I mean?' He sat back, pleased with his demonstration of an incisive and wide-ranging intellect. Then he thought of something important. 'So, Salter, yeah, go back to the college. Look for someone to help us with our inquiries. At least they'll know we're on the job and won't be so inclined to tell the newspapers. I mean, this PR woman, she's going to be pretty pleased with herself, helping the poor Indian. She might think it's a nice story for the college newspaper. Talk to her first, her and the president. Let them see what we have to be thinking if it's not a casual robbery. And find out about this guy Lyall. Was he popular? Do the students care he's gone? See what I mean? If it turns into an open file after all, let's make it a nice big one. OK?'

SALTER BEGAN WITH Barbara Czerny-Smith. 'I have to thank you for getting those kids organized,' he said. 'We've been able to establish that Henry Littledeer was somewhere else that night.'

   'And now, I suppose, you'll find some other poor devil to pin it on.'

'Fact is, what I found out by clearing Henry Littledeer leads us to think that someone set him up.'

'That's preposterous. How could anyone possibly have known he would be in the house that night?'

'He wasn't.'

She looked confused, but recovered quickly. 'That's what I *mean!* Now you'll have to find someone else.'

'In the meantime I have to assume it could have been someone close to Lyall.'

'You're just thrashing about.'

He thought of a happy image. 'Thrashing, yes, until we get to the middle of the field and the rabbits start to run. By the way, Littledeer hasn't been charged with anything yet. It's probably in his interest if you keep the story to yourself. Keep him and the college out of the papers as much as possible.'

SHREIBER WAS NEXT. Salter had come to the conclusion consulting him so much. He was also fairly sure that Schreiber would need to let the world know how close he was to the centre, and Salter planned to try to scare out a few rabbits by letting Schreiber know that the police had narrowed down their search to the Bathurst campus.

'I'm still trying to find out what sort of reputation Lyall had around here. He had a girlfriend, you told me. Was there more than one, maybe?' Salter asked.

'I thought you had it solved. Didn't we hear that a vagrant had done it?'

'We've been able to establish that the man we picked up didn't do it.'

'Some other vagrant?'

Salter tried to look like a man who was holding something back, saying nothing.

'I imagine Lyall found female company,' Schreiber said, 'I assume he wasn't celibate. I don't know who, though. I also told you that.'

'You mean no one around here?'

'I mean I don't know.'

'Who should I ask?'

Schreiber shrugged and stayed mute.

You do know, Salter thought, but you're nervous now, afraid that I'll walk around saying, 'Schreiber said...' On the other hand, it was just as likely that Schreiber knew no more than Salter, knew about Kurelek but thought that Salter didn't. 'Should I start near the top? They generally know what's going on.'

'Does this mean you think someone here did it?'

'I was told to look around here in the first place.'

'Didn't yes, the anonymous scribe. I believe you mentioned him before. Had any more?'

'Not lately.'

'Any idea who sent the first three?'

Salter smiled. 'I know who sent them. I'm just trying to figure out why. Now, what about Lyall's love-life?'

'I'd do what you suggested. Start with our vice-president and work down.'

SEVENTEEN

BUT WHEN HE RETURNED to Joan Dooley, the vice-president had a message for him. 'The president would like to see you,' she said. 'He's cleared his schedule, hoping you would come by.'

'Has he, by cracky,' Salter said, playing the rube. 'Then I'd better see him, hadn't I?'

He was surprised at the change in her in the short time since he last saw her. All the bounce seemed to have gone out of her.

'You OK?' he asked.

She nodded and shrugged at the same time, and plucked at a sheet of paper. He wondered what the president was going to tell him. She had certainly told her boss that Henry Littledeer had been cleared, which was enough to make them all realize that the on-campus investigation would start again. So President Jones would probably be putting in a strong plea for matters to be handled as discreetly as possible so as to leave the fewest scars when it was discovered that another vagrant was responsible. Fair enough.

The telephone rang and she jumped sharply, picked it up, then nodded to Salter to go across the hall to the president.

JONES'S OFFICE was almost opposite the front door of the administration building and the secretary waved him in to where the president was waiting to be interrupted. 'Thanks for putting me on the top of your list,' Jones said as he came round from behind his desk and waved Salter to a couch. 'Coffee? Yes? Coffee, Miss Wilkinson.' He sat down next to Salter. 'How are you getting along? I suppose I shouldn't ask that. I'm sorry I couldn't see you before, but it's a busy time, convocation and all that.'

He was a large man with a rugged face who obviously kept himself very fit, brimming with good-fellowship. Salter waited for him to come to the point.

'You talked to Joan, my vice-president,' Jones said. 'And she came to see me and we agreed that she may have been more discreet than she should have in the circumstances. She didn't want to gossip, so she said nothing, but we agreed that something should be said and since I wanted to talk to you anyway, I would say it.'

The coffee arrived and Salter sipped his without responding, waiting for the revelation that was coming.

'Joan didn't tell you, specifically, about a visit we had from Maurice Lyall, about a month ago?' He waited for Salter to shake his head. 'It's a chance in a million that it is relevant, but that's for you to judge, isn't it?'

'That's right.'

'Very briefly, then, Lyall came to see me because he had heard that his chances of getting the job might be affected by a relationship he had at the time with a lady.'

'Which one?'

'You must keep this in confidence.' Jones adopted what he obviously believed to be an expression of firm-minded concern for privacy.

'Maybe you'd better not tell me.' It's Schreiber, Salter thought. He's just heard from Schreiber while I was walking over here. He was pleased that he had got Schreiber right.

'What?'

'Who are we worrying about? Lyall or the lady?'

'Well, both, I suppose.'

'Why are you telling me? Because I should know? In case it matters? Then tell me. Who is this woman?'

'The lady in question is Mrs Kurelek. Judy Kurelek.'

'Her I know about. Any others?'

'You've spoken to her about...this? Did she say anything about...about how...' But he could not find the words.

'We talked. What's the problem? What was Lyall worried about? He and this Judy were lovers, and he thought that might upset you. Did it?'

'Not in the least.' Jones spoke out with vigour.

'Good. So you told him and that was the end of it.'

'Well, no. That wasn't his concern. Let me tell you what he said. Someone had whispered to him that a member of the board had heard about him and Judy and thought it was a bad idea for a dean to have a mistress on campus, especially a married woman, someone in his own division. There.'

'Is this true? I wouldn't have thought it mattered any more.'

'Of course it doesn't. I assured him that it didn't matter to me or to Ms Dooley. But the board does have power to veto, so I couldn't guarantee that he might not have received a good warning.'

'What did you advise him to do?'

'I said I would back him up whatever he did. If he wanted to brazen it out, so be it. Whatever he decided.'

'He would never know, though, would he? I mean, the board could just decide he was unqualified. They don't have to explain themselves at all, for that matter.'

'Odd you should say that. There is a bit of pressure to have a few Ph.Ds on the faculty, yes, and Maurice had abandoned his. Yes. Yes, they would never give the real reason, I imagine. You understand that all this was probably hypothetical. It was just as likely to have been someone making mischief.'

'Why didn't you find out?'

'How?'

'Ask them. The board. I'll ask them. Who are they?' Salter opened his notebook.

Jones looked embarrassed and slightly angry. 'No, no. That isn't possible.' He waved away the idea.

'So what happened?'

'I believe he gave her up. Yes, he did. He came in a week or so later and told me he had.'

'So he got the job.'

'I'm sure he would have anyway.'

'Point is, what we're concerned with here is that Judy Kurelek may not have taken it very well, and when Lyall got the job, she might have killed him. Right?' Salter paused to confirm from Jones's silence that that was exactly what the president feared. 'And when I tracked her down she might have told me why she did it.' He watched that sink in. 'And then I would ask you or Ms Dooley why you didn't tell me about

Judy Kurelek in the first place so that I could have grabbed her without a lot of clever detective work. Not very cooperative, is it? I see your point. I see why you're finally telling me. Thanks for getting around to it.'

Jones leaned back and looked away. His head began to bob under the pressure of trying to seem detached in a frightening situation. 'In my judgement, the private lives of Maurice Lyall and Mrs Kurelek were their own concern. Lyall had a right to his privacy, even in death.' He began to gabble. 'I had no idea whether the police honoured privileged conversations or even dealt in them, and if Mrs Kurelek might not suffer a severe disturbance unnecessarily. It was my understanding that you had found the criminal. But now I hear that's not the case. Ms Dooley has persuaded me that your inquiries might override considerations of privacy.'

'That's a good way to put it. When we're looking for a killer, yeah, we tend to set aside considerations of privacy. You think she might have killed Lyall?'

'Of course not. Now I've said everything I have to say and I hope you won't do any unnecessary damage.'

'Thank you, Mr Jones. If you hear or think of anything else, let me know. Right away. That way, we might avoid any more damage.'

As he left, he put his head around Joan Dooley's door. 'Thanks,' he said. She shook her head, willing him to go away. Salter did not think he had ever seen a more unhappy-looking woman. He thought he knew why. She had come across a little bit of political

hanky-panky, and she was afraid she might be impli-
cated. It confirmed his opinion that she wasn't bad;
the fact that she didn't have the balls for her job was
a good sign.

HE CALLED THE HOSPITAL and managed to get Annie, who told him that his father was asleep, that she
and May would go out to eat something, and he wasn't
needed. He went into a café on Bathurst Street, read
the morning paper for an hour, then went to see
Schreiber. 'Got it in one,' he said, cheerily. 'We were
right. All the gossip finds its way upstairs. Nice guy,
your president.'

'Oh, he is,' Schreiber said, taking the bait without
hesitation, ready with at least a paragraph. 'Our Wade
wants to retire in place. Don't-rock-the-boat-Jones, we
call him. He got a bit of a fright, I imagine, when
Jennifer Benson looked as though she might be dean,
and then that seemed to work out. Now the poor fellow has to go through it all again.'

'He seems to have to tread a fine line between the
faculty and the board. From what I gathered, the
board is more old-fashioned than he is.' Salter
grinned, sharing it with Schreiber.

Schreiber roared with laughter. 'That's our Wade,'
he said. 'The old Dickens trick. Works every time.'

'What's that?'

'The silent partner. "For myself, nothing would give
me greater pleasure, but my partner won't let me."
The fact is, the board do exactly what Jones tells them
to, but if he doesn't want to do something he blames
the board.'

'Dickens invented this game?'

'More or less.'

'What's Jones's background?'

'He's got an MA in economics. Had a career in the civil service before he came here. I believe the peak of his career was when he got to be Ontario High Commissioner for Wales or some such. When that was over they found a Royal Commission which kept him going for a couple of years, then he was out of work. There just weren't any vacancies, not even on the board of Air Canada. It was either this or nothing. So we got him.'

'Did he ever teach?'

'You mean what are his qualifications for this job? He was at Oxford for a term, so he has tone. The board is very keen on polishing our image, and he's good at that. I doubt if he killed Maurice. They got along very well.'

'Thanks. I think I found out a few things I wanted to know.' Salter stood up, nodded pleasantly, and left as Schreiber leaned forward expectantly.

JONES, THE PRESIDENT, is obviously covering his ass, Salter wrote that night. *Somebody told him about Lyall's girlfriend and he wanted the new dean to be squeaky clean. He doesn't help himself by making up little stories about Lyall coming to him. He'll get away with it if he's lucky. Apparently Lyall didn't tell Kurelek about his little chat with the president. At some point, though, Schreiber will drop her a hint, just to show he knew. What a gang! Who does Schreiber think he is, Machiavelli? Now I have to go back to*

Kurelek and find out what I should have asked before
Henry Littledeer arrived.

'YOUR HUSBAND didn't know about you and Lyall?'
he asked Kurelek the next morning.

He watched her consider lying, adding up the dan-
gers. 'Yes, he did. It was one of the factors that went
into my decision. He got an anonymous note. I denied it, of course, but he believed the note and said he
intended to find out who it was. But Maurice and I
broke up before he could. That's why I thought *I* was
in charge. I wasn't besotted with Maurice, or he with
me, and it seemed natural to end it when it got complicated. I remember now, though, who initiated the
last conversation we had. The bastard.'

'It sounds like you or Lyall had an enemy. I'll need
to talk to your husband. Do you still live together?'

'What about? He wasn't in town the night Maurice
was killed.'

It had not crossed Salter's mind that he might be
dealing with an outraged husband. 'That wasn't what
I wanted to talk to him about. I'd like to ask him
about the note. Does he still have it?'

She looked mystified and angry. 'Probably. He'll be
home at five. Here's the address.' She wrote it on a
scrap of paper and handed it to him.

'Pears Avenue,' he read. Although he had seen the
street a thousand times, he still confused it with Cot-
tingham. Both looked out on to green space.

'It runs East off Avenue Road. One block north of
Davenport.'

'The one with the food market on the corner? Sells Christmas trees?'

'Yes. Our house is down the far end.' She turned away, leaving Salter to wonder what was irritating or embarrassing about her address.

EIGHTEEN

SALTER WATCHED the house from a bench beside the tennis courts in Ramsden Park as two middle-aged hackers played out the end of their match. He realized now what had been embarrassing Judy Kurelek. The park lay between Pears Avenue and Gibson. What more natural than to go for a stroll across the grass that separated you from your lover?

A thin, fair-haired man of about fifty, dressed in academic costume—a grey tweed jacket, chinos, a white button-down collar and a striped tie appeared a few minutes after five and let himself in the front door. Salter rang the bell ten minutes later and the man opened the door immediately, evidently on his way out again. Salter showed him his card, and Kurelek said, 'What do you want?' as if speaking to a persistent nuisance.

'Five minutes.'

'About what?'

'Didn't your wife tell you?'

'I haven't spoken to her for three weeks. What do you *want?*'

Salter was tempted to say, 'Guess.' Kurelek must certainly have done so immediately. 'I'm investigating the death of Maurice Lyall. I'd like to ask you some questions. Would you mind coming down to headquarters?'

'Can't we do it here? Kurelek's voice rose out of all proportion to the situation, almost to a scream.

'Sure, but not on the doorstep.' He motioned towards the two tennis players who had finished their game and were now standing beside a car across the street, arrested by Kurelek's squawk.

Reluctantly Kurelek stepped back and led the way into the house, leaving Salter to close the door.

Salter followed him into a room furnished with objects acquired one at a time, picked up for their intrinsic interest or charm without regard for their suitability as the furnishing of a living-room. A couch or settle along one wall was from somewhere east of Suez, made of black carved wood and in its natural state only about three inches off the floor. Even with a thick pad of cushion it was only a comfortable height for dwarfs. The painted iron coffee table properly belonged in a garden, among statuary. Salter sat down in a large canvas and wood folding chair with little wooden flaps on each side. After a moment, Kurelek lowered himself on the settle and glared at Salter over his knees.

'I never knew this Lyall person,' he said. 'He used to fuck my wife. You should talk to her.' He pronounced the obscenity with depth and flourish, as though it had two syllables and several final consonants. It was evidently not part of his usual vocabulary.

'I already have.' Salter was putting together all the signs of someone slightly unbalanced, and thus unpredictable. At another level of society he would have guessed that Kurelek was dangerously but not visibly drunk, or on drugs, and would have been watching for him to pull a knife.

'Then you know all about me,' Kurelek said.

'It's the note I came about.'

'Which one?'

'I only heard of one. Were there many?'

'I think we are talking at cross-purposes. I understood you to mean the method by which I communicate with my wife.'

It took a second, then Salter said, 'You write each other notes?' He thought he had already discovered the campus author.

'Not her. Me. I told you, I haven't spoken to her for three weeks.'

Salter nodded, understanding all, thinking: He's mad. Crazed, anyway. 'I'm only interested in the anonymous note you received. Do you still have it?'

'The one that informed me that my wife was—'

'Yes.' Salter cut him off, recognizing Kurelek's need to lash himself in his situation by finding the language for what he felt. Ugly words for an ugly deed.

Kurelek opened his wallet and drew out a much-handled sheet of paper. *'Are you aware that you are currently sharing Judy's charms with another?'* the note said.

'Spelled it out, didn't he?'

'We don't know the sex of my informer,' Kurelek said.

'Can I keep this?' Salter put it away in his wallet. 'It must be obvious to you that I need a brief statement from you, in view of this.'

'About what?'

'Where were you when Lyall was killed?'

'Go fuck yourself.' Kurelek opened his arms along the back of the couch and crossed his legs in the air. He looked hard at Salter to be sure he was understood.

Salter sighed. 'You want to spend the night at headquarters, answering questions?'

Kurelek regained some control. 'All right. I apologize. But it's bad enough to know you're a cuckold, a fool, a joke, without having some great oaf of a policeman accuse you of murder.'

'I'm five foot eleven, a hundred and seventy pounds. Where were you when Lyall was shot?'

'With friends. Near Peterborough. The whole weekend. It was a holiday weekend and I couldn't stand being by myself, so a friend who teaches at Trent took me in. I came back on Tuesday morning.'

'Their name? Phone number?'

Kurelek gave him the information, adding, 'When you catch the killer, let me know, will you? I want to shake him by the hand.'

There was a sound of a key in the lock. Judy Kurelek appeared, out of breath, upset at seeing Salter already there. 'That's what I called about, Lou,' she said. 'You shouldn't have hung up.'

Kurelek rose and walked past her into the kitchen. He returned with a note which he held in two fingers. 'Finished?' he asked Salter.

'For the moment.'

'Then I shall leave you with my bride.' Kurelek dropped the note in front of his wife and walked through the front door without looking back.

She read the note and handed it to Salter. *'You will not have to suffer me much longer,'* Kurelek had written. *'It will be on your head.'*

Salter looked up, alarmed. 'This is a suicide note.'

'One of many. Sometimes two or three a day.' She crumpled the paper and dropped it on to the coffee-table. 'So you see, we don't have an open marriage.'

'You feel safe with him here?'

'I've taken advice. Apparently he's punishing me with the notes, but he isn't suicidal. I've seen a lawyer, too. As soon as I can, I'll get papers served, or whatever they do, and we'll divorce. But I don't want to push him over the edge. If I can get some normalcy into the situation I can take it from there. I can handle a few notes.'

You can't handle much more, Salter thought. 'Who else knew about you and Lyall?'

'I think now probably a lot of people, but they didn't tell me, just each other. Shirley Marconi was my only confidante—you have to have *one*, don't you?'

'It explains why she didn't vote for him.'

Kurelek smiled under her misery. 'Probably. I told her the break-up was mutual, but she didn't believe it. As I said, she thought Maurice dumped me as an embarrassment. Turns out from what you tell me that she was probably right.'

Salter stood up. 'I just came to get a statement from your husband.'

'You've had more luck than I have lately.'

ON HIS WAY DOWN the street, he passed a black, new-looking Volkswagen with a Bathurst College parking sticker. She had changed a tyre in Honey Harbour at seven in the morning. Easy to check on and therefore probably true. He looked inside to make sure it wasn't her husband's car—he hadn't checked that the Kureleks might work in the same college—but the umbrella and scarf on the back window-ledge assured him.

'YOU THINK you're on to something, Charlie, you'd better hand it over to us,' Marinelli said, the next morning.

'I'll check up on the stories, especially the Kureleks', then you can have it.'

'How's your dad?'

'That's the thing, Joe. They've already got him back to very stable again. Still confused—that's their word for doolally—but he's having little breakthroughs. He knows he's in a hospital, and he's not having violent hallucinations, but he still thinks I'm his brother. May, that's his wife, thinks she might be able to take him home soon. Annie is going to try and find a place in a convalescent hospital for a few weeks first.'

'That's great. You could be coming out of it.'

MR KURELEK HAD certainly spent the night in Peterborough. Before Salter handed over to Marinelli he would drive up to Honey Harbour to check on Mrs Kurelek's story. A phone call would do it, but he would enjoy the drive. And he had one more person he wanted to talk to, this time about Czerny-Smith.

NINETEEN

THE FORMER Mrs Lyall lived in a tiny house on Roehampton Avenue. She asked Salter to come after nine in the morning, when she would be alone.

The coat-rack in the hall spoke of a family, children, two at least. 'I remarried and we have two girls. They're at school now. My husband is at his office. He's the editor of a church newspaper.'

Both her voice and her body movements were fractionally slower than normal, like someone in a dream, and there was a faint glowing quality about her, as if she were permanently receiving very good news. Her speech was full of superlatives, gently but deliberately emphasized syllables—'absolutely'—delivered warmly but with no false notes. While they talked he listened to her seize on the good things, on the people she could be enthusiastic about. She found good in almost everyone, and where she could not, she passed. Passing, Salter soon realized, was bad.

He offered his sympathies. She shook her head decisively, insisting on honesty. 'Oh no. I hadn't spoken to Maurice for years. It's terrible, of course, and I feel sorry for... Did he have a companion?'

'I believe that ended only a few weeks before.'

'Uh-huh.' She observed two or three seconds of silence, then shook herself and put her hands in her lap, offering him a formal smile. 'What can I do?'

'I want to pick your memories. It's possible that
what happened had its roots in some college relationship in the past. This is in confidence, Mrs . . . ?'

'Gough. Hmm. I tell my husband everything.'

'I mean I will respect your confidence. Tell your
husband what you like. I'll be careful.'

'I *see*. But what happens if something I remember
makes me important to you?'

'As a possible witness? Then I may have to ask you
to make a statement. Right now I want gossip.'

'Of what kind?'

'Why did you leave your husband?'

'We disagreed on things. Moral things.'

Screwed around, thought Salter. 'Other women?'

'That, too.'

'What else?'

'How can what happened eleven years ago be relevant to your investigation?'

'If I know what kind of man he was it might help.'

'I don't want to con*demn* him. My husband says
some people are born with good instincts, and others
acquire them. But many don't.'

Salter put aside the hope that Mrs Gough would
engage in a chat about her first husband's sexual habits, and concentrated on trying to find out what else
was wrong with him. 'Did you know Jennifer Benson?' He wanted to hide his real concern in a package
of general inquiries.

'Oh, yes. *Wond*erful girl. She and Maurice worked
together forming the faculty association all those years
ago. Why are you asking about her?'

'She ran against him in the election for dean.'

'I think Maurice probably became the kind of person Jennifer has always been against. People change.' She smiled. 'But Jennifer wouldn't have changed that much. She's not an angry person, you see. A lot of the people concerned with social justice are, but sometimes you find people who will fight for the right things without losing themselves emotionally. I think they're the people who know they are bound to lose in the long run, but do it anyway. My husband's one. He never despairs because he doesn't hope for much. Jennifer's like that.'

'She only lost by one vote.'

'She would see that as a victory.'

'One of the people who voted for Lyall was Erroll Czerny-Smith. Did you know him?'

'Oh yes. I always *liked* Erroll. He and Maurice were great friends once, but not for a long time. I'm surprised that Erroll would vote for him against Jennifer. I should have thought...'

'What happened between your husband and Czerny-Smith?'

'They grew apart. Erroll stuck to his principles, but Maurice began to want power.'

Salter gritted his teeth at the cant word that was trotted out to explain what went wrong with every human relationship—sexual, social, commercial, paternal, maternal and political. In his brief career in college, all human activity had been understood as originating in the private parts including the anus; Freud was the oracle. He wondered who the guru of 'power' was and made a note to himself to ask Annie.

'You mean he was a left-winger until he got ambitious, and then became like a trade unionist looking for a government job.'

'More or less.'

'That was all?' He watched her face for signs that she might give birth to a fact, an actual incident.

'Yes. A terrible thought had crossed my mind but if Erroll supported Maurice, then I . . .' she paused.

'I need to know anything at all that might have a connection with Maurice Lyall and anyone he worked with.'

'You promised this is confidential if it is not relevant. I'm going to tell you something that you may find when you go through Maurice's old diaries. Maurice had a sexual relationship with Barbara Czerny-Smith about ten years ago, just before I left him. Sometimes these things come back long after you think they are buried. But if Erroll supported Maurice, then obviously the old incident had nothing to do with it.'

'That why you left him?' Salter said reflexively.

'You misunderstood. I'm not a puritan. I think we could have worked through that. I was more concerned with his social principles than the other thing. He seemed to be losing them.'

'This power trip?'

'Yes.'

'But the affair sounds like a pretty good reason for Czerny-Smith to have had a falling out with him.'

She shook her head. 'Erroll never knew about it at the time. Barbara asked me not to tell him, and since I had decided to leave Maurice anyway, I wanted her to have a chance of putting it behind her. Erroll was

very vulnerable. He worshipped Barbara and it would
have done a lot of damage.'

'That was very—' he wanted to say 'saintly', but the
word had a snide undertone, which was why it had
occurred to him in the face of this slightly inhuman
show of charity—'good of you. So it had nothing to
do with the friendship ending.'

She hesitated a long time before she spoke. 'Erroll
fell away from Maurice for the same reasons I did, but
it might have been accelerated by the fact that we
stopped socializing with each other. Maurice knew
why but I don't know what Erroll thought about it. I
suspect Barbara managed to find the words to rein-
force his new doubts about Maurice's ethics.'

'How long did the affair last?'

'A few weeks. Then I gather she wanted him to leave
me, so he left her instead.'

Interesting history, but old enough to be almost
certainly irrelevant. 'Wilfred Schreiber voted against
Lyall, too. Did you know him?'

She shook her head. 'He was there, but we never
had much in common.'

A pass on Schreiber, then. 'Shirley Marconi?'

'I don't know the name.'

'Judy Kurelek?'

'I never knew her then, but I've met her since. She
does volunteer work with illiterate people. A terr*if*ic
person. Was she on the committee?'

Salter shook his head and tried to recover his fum-
ble. He should have found a better way to slip in
Kurelek's name. 'No, right,' he said. 'No, I'm just
going through all Lyall's colleagues.'

'I see,' she said. 'But she's not really a colleague, is she?' Then, slightly bleakly, the glow fading a little, 'I see. She's married, too, isn't she?'

Salter tried to move past Kurelek. 'There was another candidate you might have known. Monkman.'

He was pleased to hear her burst into laughter. It cleared the air a bit and made her, for him, slightly more human. 'He should give up,' she said. 'There's nothing *wrong* with Jim. He wouldn't do any harm. But he lacks self-knowledge.' She put her hands together over her knees and looked at her feet. 'I see what you've been trying to do, Inspector. You want to know if there are any feuds you haven't heard of. I know of nothing. Apart from the husbands of any of the ladies he has enjoyed, of whom there were probably several over the years, I don't know of anyone who might have harboured a grudge.'

Now Salter judged was the right moment to return to her early reply.

'When did Erroll Czerny-Smith find out?'

'I'm sorry?'

'You said Czerny-Smith didn't know at the time that his wife was having an affair with Lyall. When did he find out?'

She looked sadly at her knees. 'I can't be sure.'

'A year later?'

'No, recently.'

'When?'

'Just before all this happened.'

'How much before?' On the whole, he thought, it might be easier if she told some lies that he could use against her, but this way, though slower, would get him there eventually.

'The same weekend. He came over here on Saturday morning, quite upset, and wanted to know if Barbara and Maurice had been lovers all that time ago. I felt quite ill, I can tell you. Even during their worst quarrel Barbara would never hurt him like that, telling him, I mean, so I asked him if Maurice had told him, and that was my mistake, you see. Maurice *hadn't* told him. Erroll had just been brooding, putting two and two together after all this time and he suddenly realized that's what happened, the reason why Barbara had wanted to break off the friendship with us.'

'Two and two? What two and two?'

She shook her head. 'There I can't help you, I'm afraid. Barbara must have said something about the old days, and then Maurice let something slip, and Erroll put it all together. Haven't you ever done that? Realized the significance of something a long time after the event? He was very upset.' She swivelled round to face him. 'But not *that* upset. He didn't do anything dreadful, I know.'

Salter's reservation showed on his face.

'I *asked* him,' she protested. 'He assured me.'

'When?'

'The day after Maurice died.'

'And you believed him?'

'He was telling the truth.'

Her simple faith in Czerny-Smith, and her insistence on testifying to his integrity, commanded Salter's respect, even if it had no value. 'When he came to you that day, did you guess what would happen? Not to Lyall. To the Czerny-Smiths.'

'I should have, but I thought they could absorb it. They've broken up, haven't they? I must call Barbara.'

'Wait a couple of days, would you?'

'TELL ME AGAIN about how the administration always wins,' Salter asked. He and Schreiber were drinking coffee, at Schreiber's suggestion, in the Lisboa, a café on Dundas, where they had come after failing to find a quiet place in the Related Studies Department. Salter wanted to ask a question without arousing Schreiber's interest.

Schreiber swelled and launched into the familiar monologue, ending, 'Don't forget, the chairman of the committee is the same person who approves their sabbatical applications. Don't want to get on the wrong side of him, or her. Essentially a strong, clever, committee chairman who is also your boss can do as he or she likes.'

'But this time, with all the vote-switching, things could have gone wrong.'

'They might have, yes.'

Salter said, 'Could Czerny-Smith just have had a change of heart?'

Schreiber's eyes sparkled. 'We'll have to wait and see. In other circumstances I would have suspected that Czerny-Smith was about to be made chairman. But I happen to know that in spite of the urgings of his colleagues, Czerny-Smith refuses to run for the chair. So what's in it for him? Change of heart, you think? Voted for the best man, you mean? I wouldn't think so. He was well known to be hostile to Lyall, called him the Vicar of Bray. No, no, I think we have to look for a deal. But not the chair. Probably, if Lyall had survived we would soon have been hearing about a new director of evening studies, a job that is at the disposal of the vice-president, doesn't require a search because it's not thought to be an academic post, more administrative. There are no faculty as such teaching full-time at night, you see, just moonlighters, so you can run it on sound business principles, on the cheap. Not immediately, of course, but a year's not long in this world.'

NOT A PROMISE, Salter wrote in his journal. Not a deal. Jennifer Benson thought the same thing but Czerny-Smith is too pure for that. A threat, maybe. Something happened between these two guys. There's a smell of blackmail. How am I going to find out? Lyall threatened Czerny-Smith, who buckled, then it stuck in his throat and he got angry enough to kill Lyall. Why? What was it? Like most innocent people, Czerny-Smith's got a flimsy alibi. How far back do these people go? They joined the college in the same year, were buddies for ten, then had a falling out. Not, says Lyall's former wife, about Barbara, because Czerny-Smith never knew. But he just found out. Did she in fact tell him about that old affair, sending him over the edge? Did Lyall tell him, maybe, and threaten to make the news public through the grapevine so that if Czerny-Smith didn't vote for him it would look like spite on his part?

Hard to believe. But could Lyall have asked for a mistrial or whatever they call it around here on the grounds that there is a conflict of interest if someone on the committee has found out you used to screw his

wife? No. Forget Mrs Czerny-Smith. Find another
scenario. Maybe he changed his vote, not to Lyall, but
away from Benson. Could she be the problem after
all?'

   I know why Lyall's first wife left him. I would
imagine he was pleased. She uses a different scale to
judge people, from 'Wonderful' to—what?— 'Needs
help,' but she sits there judging away just like the rest
of us. The result is the same, only surrounded in a
cloud of charity she pumps into the atmosphere. From
her I learned that Lyall was a sleaze and a sexual glut-
ton, that I shouldn't trust Schreiber, and that Czerny-
Smith is a wimp, all of which I knew.

TWENTY

SALTER WENT BACK to Joan Dooley for another look at the personnel files, starting with Lyall and Jennifer Benson.

She no longer reminded him that he was seeking very confidential information, but seemed eager to make sure that she was helping in every way she could.

'Was there any material in these files that the committee didn't see?'

'None whatsoever in this case. We would normally take out anything that has no bearing, and that seems very private.'

'Such as?'

She shook her head. 'Let me think of an example. Somebody might have been raised in an orphanage because his parents died in some terrible way that became very public. He might not want to be known as the survivor of that tragedy—oh gosh, I'm not doing very well making this up, but you see what I mean?'

'But these are complete, right?' He tucked them under his arm.

'You can't take them out of the office.' Her voice was strained but unwavering. 'Those files are my responsibility. Golly, I wouldn't let the Board of Governors take a personnel file away from here. No.'

Salter felt a little sorry for her. 'I could read them in the office.'

'I need someone to tell me what to do. Oh heck, all right. I'll give Melissa an hour off and you can do what you like. Wait a minute.' She picked up a phone and dialled a number, and explained to the president what Salter wanted, then put down the phone with an unhappy expression on her face. 'He says if *I* think it's the right thing to do, to go ahead. So there you are.' She called through the open door. 'Melissa, go shopping for an hour, would you? Give the inspector the key to your door.'

He read the files for three-quarters of an hour, ignoring the two fringe candidates, trying to see any problems in the files of Jennifer Benson and Lyall. Benson's file contained three major disputes she had had with the administration, disputes about her salary, her leave entitlement and about insisting on access to her office on Sundays. Otherwise it was bare.

Looking over Lyall's file again, he noticed now that one of the early inspection reports was signed by Czerny-Smith. He gave Lyall an 'Excellent' rating. Now Salter moved on to the committee members themselves and found immediately that Czerny-Smith's personnel file was missing.

He pointed this out to Joan Dooley. 'What do you want with his? He was on the committee. Oh heck, I don't know. Wait for Melissa.'

When Melissa returned, she blinked in surprise. '*I* haven't misplaced it.'

'I think you must have, Melissa. What else could have happened?'

'Somebody took the file.'

Now Dooley looked distraught. 'I'm sure no one would touch those files.' She turned to Salter. 'Melissa's very proud of her files, but I'm sure it's jammed in there someplace.'

'Somebody took it,' Melissa said. 'And I am not "proud" of my files. I just know what's in the cabinet, and when I've had something out.' She sat at her desk with a thump and started to switch on the word-processor.

Salter guessed that what he was hearing was Joan Dooley trying to ignore a potential piece of unpleasantness. 'Who else might have been looking at these files? Who might have needed to look at them?'

'Only people in senior administration with my approval. There might be a question of calculating pension rights, something like that. Sometimes we look at the files to make up a citation if we are honouring a retiree.' Now she looked wretched. 'There was a time when we had an inquiry from the RCMP about a faculty member.'

'How often are you both away from the offices without locking them?'

'Often enough. I like to keep an open door.'

'And the file cabinet isn't locked. So anyone could have come in and looked at the file.'

'Someone did,' Melissa said.

'Melissa, you don't *know* that,' Dooley cried.

'I think someone took it out, got interrupted and took off with it. *I* don't misfile things.'

'Anyone in particular?' Salter asked delicately.

But Melissa was interested only in absolving herself from a charge of carelessness. 'Could have been anyone,' she said, turning back to her desk.

They were interrupted by a phone call from Marinelli. 'We've got a sighting,' he said. 'Kid on Gibson saw a woman in the garden that night. He's home now.' He gave Salter the number.

But before he could leave, he had one more revelation to hear. 'Inspector,' Dooley said to his back as he reached the door. 'Could I have a moment?' Her voice was full of misery.

When he turned he saw that she was crying; a single tear rolled down her cheek as she looked in her purse for a tissue. Salter closed the door to the secretary's office and waited. 'I don't know how to tell you this,' she said, 'but you and I have been the biggest suckers.'

'In what way'

'Poor Maurice,' she continued. 'It's not fair. He never came to us to tell us that someone on the Board of Governors told him to break off his...relationship.' Now it was coming in a rush. 'The president did that. It wasn't even the board. It was the president.'

'But you went along with it.'

'No!!! I didn't even know! The president told *me* the same thing, that the board had told him to speak to Maurice. Then this morning he changed it around in case you had found out the truth, and asked me to back him up, if you asked me. But now I think about it, it might have been the reason...' She put her Kleenex to her face and looked in misery at Salter.

'If it's any comfort to you, Ms Dooley, I had my own ideas from the start, so your little games didn't hold me up. But what about you? What are you going to do about it?'

'Me. I'm going back to the classroom. I never should have left it in the first place.' She shook her head. 'I'm no good at this kind of thing.'

THE TREVOR FAMILY lived two houses away from Lyall. Adam Trevor sat upright in a straight-backed chair, his mother beside him. He seemed perfectly composed for a ten-year-old talking to a policeman. His mother said, 'Adam was sick on the night of the . . . incident. He was in bed in his room. Then he went on a student exchange trip to Quebec City.'

'Actually,' the boy said. 'It was just outside Quebec City, though we did visit Quebec City.'

Mrs Trevor continued. 'This morning at breakfast we were all talking about Mr Lyall and about you coming round the other day, and he said . . . you go on, Adam.'

'I saw a lady in a white raincoat with high-heeled shoes and a scarf on her head and sunglasses crossing the back garden while I was watching the fireworks.'

'You read detective stories, son?'

'I watch them.'

'He writes them,' his mother said, half-wonderingly, half proudly.

'Just small ones. I'll show them to you. I've written hundreds of them.'

'Maybe later. Could I see the bedroom?'

The boy jumped down. 'I'll show him, Mum.'

Salter followed Adam up to the second floor, to a small bedroom at the back of the house. The narrow bed was under the window. 'Were you in bed at the time?'

'I had a fever of a hundred and two.'

'Were you lying down?'

'Not properly.' The boy leaped on to the bed and composed himself in the position, semi-horizontal, propped up with two pillows under his head so that he could see through the window.

'Can we change places?' Salter asked. He climbed gingerly on to the small bed and put himself in the boy's position, his feet dangling over the end of the bed. 'You can't see the whole garden from here. Which way did she walk?' The tree in the lane was outside his field of vision.

'I could see her. She came out of the back of the house and walked across to the gate, then sort of ran off down the lane. I watched her the whole way.'

'Anything else about her? Any idea how old she was?'

'Quite old. Like Mum. I thought it *was* Mum at first.'

Between thirty and fifty, Salter thought. 'And that was all you saw?'

'I did see her, didn't I?'

'Indeed you did, and that's very helpful, but you didn't see anything after that? How long did you watch the fireworks?'

'Not long. I fell asleep. I was feverish. I had a temperature of a hundred and two.'

'You're a good witness.'

Adam accepted this, and they went downstairs. Salter thanked Mrs Trevor for calling so promptly.

'He made me,' she said, pointing to Adam.

'What's your name?' Adam asked. 'In case I think of anything else.'

Salter gave him a card.

'Staff Inspector is like Chief Inspector?'

'Sort of.'

'Can I watch you work some time?'

'I sit in an office. There's not much to see. But give me a call in a couple of weeks and I'll show you round the police museum.'

'I'd rather see the computer.'

'Computer it is, then.'

SALTER LEFT the Trevors and let himself into Lyall's house. He moved directly to the centre of the maze, to the desk, and to the drawer with Lyall's personal files. He found nothing. Then he realized that what he was looking for was more personal than personal, was 'secret' in fact, not to be left in a place where it might be found by his cleaning lady or his mistress. Trying not to be too clever about it, he looked in the obvious places, then turned to the cabinets containing Lyall's academic papers. Once, he remembered, he had bought some earrings for his wife to surprise her at Christmas, long before the event, and hidden them so well that he never did find them. Occasionally, daydreaming, he would still be visited by a sudden memory of where he had put them and run upstairs and unroll all the thick socks he used for fishing in October, or empty out his binocular case, but he never found them. Now, wondering where the best place would be to hide a file the possession of which would ruin you if discovered, Salter considered all the possible hiding-places and for all of them found an emergency which might uncover the file (a fire or a robbery would do it for most of them), and on a very old principle decided that the safest place was among the academic papers, with a lot of other files.

There were four drawers to go through, but the administration's personnel files were different in colour from Lyall's own files, orange instead of buff, and different in kind, simple folders, unlike Lyall's hanging files, so that by taking out a handful of Lyall's files Salter created the room to be able to flick the others along the side-bars very rapidly, looking for the odd one out. He found Czerny-Smith's file in the second drawer where Lyall, probably not wanting to rely totally on his memory, had filed it in the right alphabetical place between 'Confederation' and 'Dominion Status'. He skimmed it quickly for any extraordinary revelations and, finding none, borrowed a large envelope from Lyall's stationery drawer to reserve the file for a more leisurely look in the hospital that night. He looked at his watch. Honey Harbour was too far to get to in what was left of the day. He would go up first thing in the morning.

TWENTY-ONE

HONEY HARBOUR is located in old Ontario cottage country. On this part of the Georgian Bay the cottages tend to be well-kept and expensive, a long way up-market from the fishing shack a hundred miles farther north that Salter used occasionally. He found the service station on Highway 69 without any trouble, and thought through his scenario while he was getting filled up. The probable owner of the station was standing in the doorway of a service bay. Salter pulled over to a parking space outside the coffee shop and approached him. 'I'm trying to track down a friend of mine,' he said. 'She's staying in a cottage owned by a family named Pride. She left a tyre off here to be fixed after the long weekend.'

'Still here.'

'The tyre?'

'The wheel. In the back.' He pointed his chin over his shoulder. 'Daryl!' he bellowed. 'That woman pick up that wheel yet? Slashed tyre?'

'It's in the back,' Daryl shouted.

'In the back,' the owner repeated.

'Is it fixed?'

'Can't fix a sucker like that. Hadda put a new one on.'

'That bad?'

'Slashed. Fucking Indian kids.'

'Can I have a look?'

'What at? The new tyre? Threw the old one out. She owes me a hundred and twenty. Daryl! Bring that wheel out, will you? You want to take it? Pay for it? She called me she wouldn't be back till after the black flies. I was going to drop it off when I was in the city. You want to take it? Hundred and twenty, plus GST.'

Daryl appeared, wheeling the tyre.

Salter produced a credit card. 'Sure.' He bent down to examine the wheel, running his finger round the inside of the rim. He straightened up and signed for the bill while Daryl put the wheel in the trunk of his car. 'How long was she going to drive around without a spare?' he asked disapprovingly. 'She left it off with you in the morning, didn't she? After the weekend?'

'S'right. The Prides, they went out the night before, but she stayed over on her own. Them Indian kids probably thought the place would be empty and they could pick it over. When they found her still there, they got pissed off and slashed her tyre.'

'I guess she figured she could make it. It's a pretty new car.'

'The Volvo? Not that new. They last a long time, them suckers. Daryl! Pump!'

BACK IN THE CITY, he called Marinelli to tell him what he had found. Marinelli said, 'If you're going to arrest her, take someone with you. Regulations.'

'I'll call if I need help. I want to poke around a bit more first.'

He drove to Bathurst College and established that the faculty all parked in one of two parking lots. There were no guards on the barriers, which were operated by magnetic cards. There were three Volvos in the first lot and he examined each closely. In the second lot there was just one. He took the licence numbers into the administration office and asked for the names of the owners. When he had these, he began to get some idea of what had gone on.

He parked on Pears Avenue behind Judy Kurelek's car and spent a few minutes looking at her wheels. Then he knocked on the door. 'I've brought your tyre back,' he said. 'Shall I put it in your trunk?'

She started to speak, then stopped, and backed away. He followed her into the house, closing the door behind him. 'Your husband home?'

She shook her head and collapsed on to the dwarf's couch. He took the chair opposite and made a business of getting out his notebook and making himself comfortable.

'How did you know where it was?' she asked, very quietly.

'You told me. Remember? The service station just before the Honey Harbour road. Where you left it off that Tuesday morning.'

She was recovering now, hoping it was nothing. 'Were you just passing by?'

'Oh no. That's what I went up there for. To look at the tyre.'

'And?'

'I found out you were lying.'

'What are you talking about? Didn't you ask the service station? I left it there at seven in the morning.'

'I know that. When did you realize it was flat?'

She made a show of thinking. 'As soon as I tried to drive away from the cottage. I was all loaded up, but as soon as I sat in the car I could feel something was wrong.'

'But you drove it anyway? Five miles to the service station?'

'I changed it, of course.'

Salter had the elementary lie he was looking for. 'There's no sign of a wheel being changed on your car. That was a spare that was slashed. It's still got the original dust on it. I think you slashed it yourself when you drove back up to Honey Harbour that night to give yourself an alibi. You don't have much experience with alibis. The best ones are the ones we can't check on.'

'That's preposterous.'

'Is it? Next door to Maurice Lyall's house lives a ten-year-old boy. He was watching the fireworks that night from a bedroom window. He's a very observant kid and he saw a woman leave Lyall's house and cross the garden into the alley. As I say, he's a very good witness and he could make a pretty good identification. Has done.'

He held his breath. It was all literally true, but what he was trying to do depended on his guessing correctly why she had created the false alibi, after the event.

'I still don't know what you are talking about.'

'Whose car did you borrow?'

Now she stayed silent.

Salter said, 'The tyre I brought down from Honey Harbour belonged to a Volvo. You own a Volkswagen. I knew you were lying before I went up there because your car doesn't have a spare. It has a little wheel that'll get you to a service station. So whose car did you borrow, and why? Come on.' He spoke to her as if she were a child he had caught out in an elementary fib.

Still she said nothing.

'What's Shirley Marconi's number?' he asked, getting up.

'She's not involved.'

'With what? What's her number? She must know why you drove up to Honey Harbour at three in the morning and set up the tyre alibi. It's her car you used. What did you tell her?'

'She was only trying to help me.'

'Let's have it all now.'

Her eyes followed an invisible object round the room, swerving past him. 'I didn't kill Maurice,' she said at last. 'Nor did Lou.'

'What *did* you do that night? I know where he was.'

She looked for answers in the weave of her skirt as she spread it over her tightly-clamped knees. 'I decided to spend Monday night at the cottage by myself. My hosts had already gone but I didn't want to buck the traffic on Monday night. Highway 69 is impossible at the end of a holiday weekend.'

'Then you changed your mind.'

She nodded her head up and down, as if being forced. 'I was afraid of what he might do.'

'Lyall?'

'Lou. My husband. I didn't know he had gone away. I'd had another note before I left and I got to thinking what it would seem like if he was serious this time and I had just gone away for the weekend and not bothered.'

'He threatened suicide again?'

'Yes.'

She seemed to think she was finished. Salter prodded her on. 'What time did you come down?'

'I got back around ten-thirty Monday night. There was another note on the kitchen counter, but no sign of Lou.'

'Do you still have it?' Salter held out his hand.

She shook her head.

'What did it say?'

'"*You have destroyed my life, and now I'm going to destroy his.*" I went right over there.'

'How many notes was he sending you?'

'There was one every day, at least. He even sent them in the mail. To his own house. I found one in my purse. In the coffee-pot.'

'All with the same message?'

'At first they were about how I was killing him. Then they started to talk about revenge. So when I saw this one . . .' She stopped.

'You thought he had gone to kill Lyall?'

She nodded.

Salter waited.

'What else do I have to tell you?' Her voice was beginning to break.

'Tell me how you found him.'

'He was on the floor by the bed.' She gave a convulsive heave. 'He was sort of mixed up with the bed-

clothes. His face was all right but . . . he'd been shot in
the body. In the middle. The room smelt horrible.'

'It always does. Did you touch him?'

'No-o.' She relived the scene. 'His eyes were open.'

'Where was the gun?'

'On the floor in the middle of the room.'

'Did you leave it there?'

'No,' she whispered. 'I cleaned it off with a guest
towel from the bathroom. One of those paper ones. I
flushed that down the toilet. And I put the gun back
near him. I sort of threw it down because I didn't want
to get any blood on me.'

'Why did you do that?' Salter raised his voice to
prevent her drying up completely.

'I thought I might make it look as if he did it himself.'

'Did you go then?'

'No. I realized that there weren't any fingerprints on
the gun now, not even Maurice's, and I thought of
pressing his fingers against it. But I couldn't touch
him.'

'You wouldn't have got them right, anyway. Then
what?'

'I thought I could still make it look like a burglary.
So I went into all the other rooms, emptying out all the
drawers. I made myself take his watch off, and I took
it and the money in the drawer and the tray and filled
up his briefcase and hid them under a tree in the lane.
I covered it up with some leaves so it's probably still
there.'

'You know we charged someone with the homicide, do you? An Indian?'

'I had nightmares about it, but you let him go, didn't you?'

'I think he had a few bad nights himself. You remember how you left the house? Did you go straight to the tree?'

'I think so.'

'It's not the kind of thing you forget, Mrs Kurelek. Give me a piece of paper.'

She stumbled into the kitchen and came out with a message pad and pencil, slumping back on the settle.

Salter drew a poor sketch of the back of Lyall's house, the garden and the tree. 'Now draw me a dotted line of the route you took when you left the house.'

She thought about it for long enough to grip the pencil firmly, then traced a straight line of dots from the house to the tree.

Salter put the sketch in his pocket. 'Then what?'

'Then I came home across the park.'

'And?'

'I waited until one o'clock. About then I started to telephone, to see if I could find Lou. I called you people, and some hospitals, and then I called the two or three people he might have gone to. When I called his friends in Peterborough, they told me he was there. He'd been with them all weekend.'

'Then you had a problem, didn't you? Do you remember what you thought then?'

'That's when I thought it might have been a burglar who got frightened and ran away.'

'No one else cross your mind?'

'No, no one. No one.'

'Then what?'

'Then I called Shirley.'

'Did you think she'd done it?' By her face he could tell she had.

'Of course not. I needed to talk to someone. She came right over and we talked for a long time, then we thought of giving me this alibi. She knew I hadn't killed Maurice, but she said no one would believe me, so I drove up to Honey Harbour with the spare tyre.'

'Hers.'

'Yes. I didn't know until then that I don't have a spare. She told me that. So I took her car.'

The assistance of Shirley Marconi made it believable, just. Once her friend had accepted that she had not killed Lyall, then all the Nancy Drew instincts would come into play, concocting the silly alibi.

He stood up. 'You've committed a crime, of course, and you'll be charged. Let's start by going down to headquarters and getting your statement.'

'I didn't kill Maurice.'

'You've got a good story, but you've had time to work on it. Even if it's true, you're some kind of accessory, as is your pal. They'll know down at headquarters.'

On the way, she said, 'What made you look at my tyre?'

'That was your bad luck. I saw your car parked on the street, and I noticed that none of the wheels looked as if it had been changed lately. Then I realized that you don't have a spare, just one of those dinky little wheels. So it had to be another car. See, I believed your story, at first. But once I got thinking about it, I realized how dumb it was, even if you had a flat, to leave it at Honey Harbour and go without one until the worst of the mosquitoes were gone. Two weeks? A month? I mean, if you're happy to drive to Toronto without a spare, then it makes sense to bring it down with you and get it fixed locally. It was dumb, or clumsy. Then I realized that you and the cleaning lady were the only people who knew about the money in the drawer. We found the money, by the way.'

'Under the tree?'

'More or less.'

TWENTY-TWO

To Marinelli, he said, 'She's telling the truth. She wouldn't wear high heels in cottage country or to drive home, and why would she change to run across the park to see Lyall? She was trying to get there before he was killed. And whoever the kid saw didn't go near the tree and was probably there an hour earlier. Truth is, it was probably a neighbour taking a short cut home— you can't actually see Lyall's back door from the kid's bed—but it put me on to Judy Kurelek. I'll get statements from the only other woman with a cause, Jennifer Benson, who lost out in the vote, but I think it was a neighbour. And I'll tell you why. The kid says it looked like his mum from the back. Jennifer Benson doesn't. She's got a very big bum.'

'This Kurelek woman. She seems pretty cool, wiping the gun and trashing the house and all.'

'OK, she could have done it, but you'll have to find some clothes of hers with powder on them. Her story is cool, I grant you, but remember she's married to a goddam madman who leaves death threats in the tea-pot. I can see why she would believe that he'd finally flipped. It put her in a panic. You may be right about another robber after all.'

But that evening he studied Czerny-Smith's file for an hour until he felt he could have written the man's biography. Most of the information was financial, concerned chiefly with how much Czerny-Smith had accumulated in his pension fund. There were two requests for sabbatical leave, one to make a 'study tour of technical colleges in England', the other to compile a collection of essays suitable for use as a teaching tool at Bathurst College. Both had been granted, and Czerny-Smith had filed a report on the year's work in each case. The essays had been collected and edited, and a little introduction written, but no publisher had been found for the project because Czerny-Smith had been unable to persuade any of the other colleges in the system to adopt it. Anything there? Salter wondered. It seemed an ideal way to spend a year doing a week's work, but was the fact that Czerny-Smith had never got it published a black mark? And why did he have to go to Aix-en-Provence to do it?

There were several reports by his colleagues on his teaching, all of them in laudatory language. Salter suspected they were written in code. Only a colleague would know how to interpret a sentence like, 'Although the students seemed unprepared, Mr Czerny-Smith managed to plant some seeds which I am sure will flourish,' or, 'Mr Czerny-Smith showed the flexibility of an old hand in switching from the lecture mode he had prepared to a tutorial style, and those students who appeared got the benefit of some very individual instruction.' The sum of the reports had been favourable enough to grant him tenure.

That night he said to Annie, 'I'm missing something.'

'Maybe it's missing from his file.'

Salter remembered Joan Dooley's comment about protecting the information in the file if there was anything which justified an extra level of discretion. His training made him perform the obvious chore of phoning his office and asking them to check on the possibility that Czerny-Smith's secret, if it existed, was criminal.

'If it's too long ago, then it's wiped out,' the clerk reminded him.

Except, Salter thought, in the academic world. 'Have a look,' he urged. He turned back to Annie. 'Know any discreet professors?'

She laughed. 'What about that gang you met at Douglas College? Why?'

'I need a code-breaker. I'm missing something in front of my face. That's it. The cockney shouter. What was his name? Usher. He might be the one. He'd keep his mouth shut.'

'Would he do it?'

'He won't want to, which is why he's the best person to try.'

Seth appeared through the door, looking for something to eat. 'How's Grandad?' he asked.

'I'm just on my way down to relieve May,' Salter said. 'She hasn't called, so he can't be any worse.'

Annie brought a bowl of clam chowder to the table for Seth, and disappeared into the basement to tend to the laundry.

'Want me to go?' Seth asked. 'You take me down and bring May back. I can come home on the subway.'

'You don't mind?'

Seth shook his head. 'I'll read him bits from the *Globe.*'

There was a long, long pause before Salter spoke until it was clear that a large subject was about to be broached. Salter looked at Seth's bowl, and Seth watched his father over the edge of each upraised spoon.

'You get along well with him,' Salter said eventually.

'Sure. Ever since I taped his stories when I was in Grade Ten.'

'But you still see him.'

'I call in if I'm in the area. He likes to see me, I guess. Still gives me a dollar for candy.'

'I wish I found him that easy.'

Seth spooned out the last of the chowder and cleaned his bowl with a piece of bread. 'It's easier for me. I'm not his son. I mean, it's easy for me to just like him.'

Salter struggled with this. 'I like him, Seth. I like him, but he doesn't know it.'

'Mind if I say something, Dad? I don't think you do. You love him, sure, but you don't like him as much as you think you should. So you feel guilty about it. You shouldn't. You do what's right. You and Mom.'

'She does, that's for sure.'

'When did you and Grandad kind of go different ways? At my age?'

'Before that.' Salter put his cup in the sink and returned to sit opposite his son. 'We never had much going for us after I was sixteen. I grew away and never grew back. It might have been different if my mother hadn't died.'

'He's lucky to have May.'

'He is, isn't he? I haven't done enough for him, though.'

'Not a lot you can do about it now. Anyway, I think you're wrong. I remember him when I was a kid, before we got to be buddies. He used to come over here and upset everybody, including Mom. Nothing for you to feel guilty about. That's just the way it is.'

The word 'guilty' was the clue. This was coming from somewhere else, from some previous discussion. He would pick it up later. Now, he said, 'Why did you say "my age"?'

'When?'

'Just now. You asked did Dad and I grow apart at your age?'

'Because that's as old as I am. It hasn't happened to you and me yet, has it? I was wondering what to expect.' He stood up and finished his glass of milk. 'It was a dumb thing to say, sorry. Don't start worrying about *us,* Dad. What's gone down between you and Grandad is just bad luck, Fate, or something. It's different around here. We got lucky,' he ended cheerfully. 'Now I'll get my coat and we'll skedaddle.'

IN BED THAT NIGHT, Salter picked up the sign he had got from Seth. 'You've been talking to Seth about me,' he said.

A pause. Then: 'We've been worried. I have.'

'Isn't he a little young to be analysing me?'

'He's old enough to see the obvious.'

'With your help.'

'I need someone to talk to, too.'

'He said . . . he said he doesn't have my problem.'

Annie rolled sideways on to him and put her hand on his belly. 'We talked about that. I thought that one of the things that might be bothering you was whether this father/son thing is inevitable, if it would happen to you and the boys. I didn't think it was, if it hasn't happened already. After I explained it to Seth, he didn't either. Now you don't. But maybe you should talk to someone else. You can't trust me. I'm too involved.'

'You don't like him.'

'Don't say that. Say I've resented him for your sake. And I've talked to Seth about that, too, to see what it looked like to him.'

'Jesus. You've covered a lot of ground between you. My son, the shrink. I guess I should call myself lucky.'

'We all are.'

He felt himself collapse within as if he had just scrambled up a steep cliff to safety. Then he stretched out in a racking physical preparation for the languor that was coming and felt his penis reach up and touch her fingertips. She left her hand there, waiting, but almost immediately he shrank again. 'Reflex,' he said, 'stress', and pushed her over so that her back was to him, spooning her into him. 'Remember we used to be able to sleep like this?'

She grunted. 'You OK?'

'I'll manage. You're right, of course. For a while I was beginning to wonder if I should go out and buy a couple of drums so that Seth and I could have a ses-

sion, naked, in the woods, looking for each other. I
won't bother now.'

PROFESSOR USHER opened the door of his apartment
and grinned at Salter. 'It's himself,' he shouted. 'Salter
of the Yard.'

This was exactly why he had asked if he could call
on Usher at home. Usher was a clown and a shouter
who found the world entertaining and reacted bois-
terously to it, but as Salter had learned before, he was
fundamentally miserable when confronted with misery, secure in himself and uninterested in identifying
the faults of others, and intelligent. In the investigation of the death of one of his colleagues a few years
before, he had clearly been made uncomfortable by
the evidence of strife and backbiting among his colleagues that Salter had uncovered. Salter had been left
with a very strong impression of active goodness un-
derneath a refusal to be solemn. It occurred too him
now that Usher was at the other end of the spectrum
from Wilf Schreiber; he was aware of human frailty,
but he had no taste to enjoy it. But he *was* noisy.

As Salter entered the living-room, he found that
Usher came by his style naturally. As Usher guided
him to a seat, a woman's voice came from the bathroom. 'Raymond, you've left this diaper in the bath-
tub. Why did you do that? You know I am in a hurry
and I haven't time to deal with it now. You must deal
with it yourself.'

Salter wondered what nationality lay behind the
accent and the careful, unidiomatic diction.

'Agatha, I don't know what to do with shitty diapers,' Usher shouted back, in a way that would have
had Salter's wife descend on him with a blunt instru-
ment but turned out to be ordinary discourse in this
house. Another voice joined in, a girl's. 'Mummy, I
need desperately to go to the toilet, and Jonathan has
been in there for hours. What are you doing, Jonathan?'

'That's very rude, Jennifer,' came the muffled voice
of Jonathan from behind the door. 'Since you ask,
I'm having a movement.'

'While you're waiting, get Chloe dressed, Jennifer.
That would be a help instead of standing in the hall
complaining all the time,' Mrs Usher shouted.

There was a pounding of tiny feet and a naked girl
child of perhaps eighteen months ran through the living-room and into a bedroom, shrieking with glee,
followed by a girl of about sixteen. Jonathan, perhaps fourteen, appeared, buckling up his belt, shouting 'The throne is vacant, Jennifer.'

'I'm sorry,' Usher said in a gabble. 'My wife refuses to use disposable diapers and Chloe is not quite
trained yet. And these two always fight about the toilet every morning. Now Jonathan, help Jennifer with
Chloe and get out of here. Go on, sod off, the lot of
you. I have a guest.'

'Charlie Salter,' Salter said quickly before Usher
could identify him by rank and profession.

The boy put out his hand. 'I'm Jonathan, that was
Jennifer, and the infant is Chloe. She is a product of
my parents' middle-aged passion.'

'Mr Salter doesn't want to know that,' Mrs Usher said now, appearing in the doorway. 'Go to school.' She was Chinese, or looked it to Salter, a tall, slender woman, dressed for the street in a cotton dress and sandals. Clearly a love match, Salter thought. What else could bring together this little Englishman, so heavily bearded, side-burned, and moustached that only his nose and his thick-lensed glasses showed through, and this attractive Oriental lady?

'Should I come back?' he wondered to Usher.

'No, no. This lot will be gone in a moment.'

It took fifteen minutes for the noise of battle to fade along the corridor. Then Salter said, 'First of all, I need to know if I can speak in confidence.'

'No, no,' Usher said grinning. 'No secrets here. Sorry.'

'I need some advice that may affect a man's life.'

'I expect you do, but I can't swear to keep a confidence about something I know nothing about. You tell me something I think this man ought to know, and I'll tell him. I have higher allegiances than yours, Inspector.' Usher seemed to retreat behind the thickness of his glasses.

'I won't ask you to do anything illegal, or even immoral. I need some help.'

'All right, but if this information turns out to put this man in one of the many categories you think illegal, but I think are nobody's business except his, then you won't get any help from me.' Usher continued to grin, but in a way that emphasized his seriousness.

'I don't think that will happen.' Salter pondered and took a breath. 'This guy may have killed someone.'

'Let's not waltz each other round the garden any more. What do you want me to do?'

'Read this file. Tell me if there's anything wrong, strange or missing.' Salter handed it over. 'Do you know him?' he added, guessing that at the academic level, Toronto was a small town.

'No.'

'He's an instructor at Bathurst College.'

'Ah. So what I'm looking for is an incriminating letter. No. You would have found that. Faculty association accused him of perpetrating a defalcation and you want translation? No. What then?'

'I don't know. Somebody borrowed this file illegally, and I can't ask anyone at Bathurst for help for the reasons you've just given, and because I know who borrowed it. There may be something in there which has nothing to do with me but would make a difference if those people saw it. Or one of them.'

Usher weighed the orange folder in his hand. 'I'll read your file,' he said. 'I'll read it tonight. Come by tomorrow after lunch. I teach until twelve and this gang won't be home in the afternoon.'

USHER WAS WAITING for him the next afternoon. He made Salter some dark orange tea and opened the file on his lap.

'Nothing,' he began. 'All bumpf. Unexamined life of quiet desperation. No incriminating letters. Nothing.' He closed the file and offered it to Salter.

'Nothing,' Salter repeated and waited for the 'except' that was evidently coming, if he waited long enough.

'The only thing I could see that might even be missing was a confirmation of his graduate degree. Doesn't mean a damn thing. I don't think I bothered to send mine up. Probably wiped Chloe's bum with it. Go through the files and you'll find a lot of them are missing. The college takes your word for it, as they bloody well should, and then everybody forgets.'

Salter opened the file to the first document. 'What are we talking about? Which degree?'

Usher jumped up and walked into the kitchen, shouting over his shoulder. 'He did an MA at York. Look at his original job application. It's dated March the something. Look at the section marked "Education". The degree was to be awarded in May. He got the job and never bothered to send forward the confirmation.'

'But he got the degree?'

'It was a course degree, no thesis required, and he was just finishing up the last course when he applied at Bathurst.'

'What if he didn't?'

'What does it matter? He got the job. He's done it for twenty years. People abandon higher degrees all the time. The Americans have a name for it. "ABD," they call it, "All But Dissertation".'

'At the MA level? Is there a name for an unfinished MA?'

'Not that I've heard, but people generally do finish the MA, especially the kind without a dissertation. Graduate schools give them away, practically. Anyway, if you check I'm sure you'll find plenty of people at Bathurst with BA's. We have some at Douglas though we don't hire them any more. We're very status conscious, nothing but bloody doctors, now. Thank God I got in in time.' Usher laughed loudly.

'You don't make any distinction?' Salter looked for the right question. Usher was dodging, but he wouldn't lie if cornered.

'Not the slightest.'

'You all get paid the same?'

'In the end, yes.'

This was it. 'In the beginning?'

'I think at Douglas we start the doctors off an increment higher, something like that. Probably not at Bathurst.'

'I'll have to check. How can I find out if the degree was awarded?'

'There are records. The degrees awarded are published every year.'

'Where will I find them? Who will I ask?'

Usher took the file from Salter and spoke into it, quietly. 'I already did. I foresaw you clumping around York, flashing your police card, demanding a check on whether one Erroll Czerny-Smith had actually been awarded his bloody degree and clouding what has obviously been a very valuable career. So I cancelled my classes and went out to York this morning and confirmed through a pal of mine without anyone knowing what I was up to that the records do not show that he finished his degree—there is an essay outstanding or some such rubbish—so his transcript is still marked "incomplete", though they wouldn't let him make it up after a certain time, certainly not now. He would have to begin again, I suspect.'

'If this is true, and Bathurst teachers have a contract like yours, he's been overpaid for twenty years.'

'Just one increment at most. What are you going to do about it?'

'I don't know. I'm not concerned with how much he was paid, unless that turns out to be why a man was killed.'

'If it doesn't?'

'Maybe they don't have the same contract as you people. I'll have to check. You didn't do that, too, did you?'

'I thought of it, but I don't have any pals at Bathurst.'

Salter closed the file. 'I'll have to get a copy of the contract.'

Usher put his head in his hands. 'I may have buggered up a man's life,' he said quietly.

'So far you may have been just the man to help me avoid buggering it up if it's not necessary. That's why I came to you. I wanted help from someone who wouldn't gossip.'

'Would you let me know?'

'I'll tell you what the contract says.'

AN HOUR LATER Salter was in possession of the Bathurst faculty contract. He did not bother to give his reasons to Joan Dooley, fairly sure she would speculate and guess wrong. He also looked at the college calendar for the year after Czerny-Smith arrived, and one or two others over the years. When he was satisfied, he called Usher. 'Professor? You'll be glad to know that Bathurst is a lot more democratic than your gang. They don't pay for degrees. They like them, but they don't buy them. They pay for experience. It made no difference to our man's pay at all.'

'Then what I told you won't help your investigation?'

'Probably.' Salter let it stand for the negative, too.

For he would have to tackle Czerny-Smith and shake the truth free. Whatever might have happened between Lyall and him was known only to Czerny-Smith now. Salter looked back through his journal and noted the flimsiness of Czerny-Smith's alibi and the guess he had made at the time that its flimsiness meant that it was probably a good one. It was time to abandon that. The flimsy alibi was the only weapon he could use to pry open the truth. He would have to use the same tactics he had used with Judy Kurelek and for that he would need to tackle the Czerny-Smiths at home.

'Inspector Salter. Your wife called.' Melissa looked at a slip of paper in her hand. 'She wants you to meet her at the hospital.'

'Is she there now?'

'She was in a hurry. She just left a message.'

TWENTY-THREE

HE'S DEAD, he thought. I've lost my chance. All the trite phrases and self-justifications came to mind—'I didn't even get to speak to him. He never knew me at the end. I did see him last night, though. He seemed all right then. Best I've seen him—' followed by all the questions about the practical problems. His father had not been near a church for at least fifty years, but somewhere in the past he was descended from Anglicans. Where do you hold the service these days—in the funeral parlour? What about May? Maybe she was religious, in which case perhaps she would want him buried from her church. Should Angus come back from the Island? He was never close to his grandfather, unlike Seth. And afterwards? Let there be a wake, he thought. That winter he had attended a funeral of a relative of Annie's, on a bitter, sleety day with a minister who had never heard of the dead person. Afterwards, looking for a drink, the mourners had shared a pot of tea and two packets of Peek Frean's biscuits in a cheerless ante-room of the funeral parlour, and then slunk home. No, by Christ. If May didn't mind, they would have a wake at his house and get royally pissed, even sing a bit. Something, anyway. And then take May away with them for a few days. Not to the Island. To Washington to see the tulips or whatever it was people went to Washington to see. She had made the old man happy for ten years.

He pulled in to the parking lot of the hospital, and ran into the lobby, his face frozen from the effort of holding on to himself. Up on the ward, Annie was standing in the door of the room, and she ran forward to stop him. 'Be careful what you say,' she warned. 'May's in there with him now. It's her decision, and I think she should have her way.'

'What's to decide? Of course. Whatever she wants. What?'

'She's taking him home.'

Salter sat down on a bench in the corridor. 'He's not dead?'

'Oh, Charlie. I'm sorry. I should have left a better message. He's had quite a recovery. Not physically, but mentally. When he woke up this morning he knew where he was and immediately said he wanted to go home. The doctor says he can in a few days. He wants to go now. I thought you might be able to persuade him to rest for a bit until he's stronger, and we can arrange for home help.'

Salter got up and walked into his father's room. The old man was propped up in bed, holding May's hand.

'Well, look who's here,' his father said. 'Finally. Nice of you to bother.'

'He's been here every day,' May said. 'Like me.'

'Don't try to keep the peace, May. He hasn't bloody been *near* me. None of them have.' He thought for a moment. 'Except Seth. *He* cares.'

'Now stop it,' May said. She turned to Salter. 'He's not quite himself yet.'

'He seems to be.'

'Now,' the old man said.

'The doctor said in a couple of days.'

'I'm all right. I want to go now.'

'I won't take the responsibility,' Salter said.

'You don't have to.' Then the tiny access of strength drained away. 'May will look after me,' he croaked.

'In a couple of days.'

May said, straightening the bedcovers, 'He's right. Couple more days and we'll have you home. Sooner the better. People die in these places.'

Defeated, the old man turned away in disgust and closed his eyes. Then he opened them briefly and painfully turned his head to look at Salter. 'Seth was here,' he said.

SETH WAS WAITING by the nursing station. As he went towards the room, Salter stopped him. 'Did you see him already?'

Seth nodded cheerfully.

'He's asleep now. We can come back later.'

The three of them left the hospital. In the parking lot, Annie said, 'I got a cab. May called me because she was afraid he would discharge himself. Apparently he woke up feeling very strong.'

He got into the car and waited for Annie. Seth embraced his mother and said something which made her smile. He leaned close to the car and patted his father on the head. 'See you later, Pop. Take it easy.'

'What did he say?' Salter asked.

'He said, "He'll be all right now."'

'He does look a lot better, doesn't he?'

'Seth meant you.'

AN HOUR and a large Scotch later he was in Marinelli's office.

'Any news?' Marinelli asked.

'The old bastard's recovering. He's going home in a couple of days.'

Marinelli, embarrassed, said, 'I meant about the case.'

'Oh, that. Yeah. I think I'll wrap that up tonight.'

'That's great. Just like that? Can you let me in on it?'

'He woke up this morning fighting with the nurses, trying to go home. His head's all back in place. He even knew me enough to bitch at me.'

'That's great, too. Are you going to make an arrest?'

'What? I doubt it. Not tonight. They aren't going to run away. Be on your desk tomorrow.' Salter stood up and slapped Marinelli's desk. 'I've got to find a place for them closer to us, so we can keep an eye on him.'

'Yeah? He might have something to say about that. By the way, there's a message from the CPIC guy. Someone called Czerny-Smith was picked up on May 24 for drunk driving and spent the night in the Don Jail. He one of your seven suspects?'

'Jesus Christ.' Salter stared at Marinelli, then started to laugh. 'I was just about to arrest him.'

And then he guessed what was going on.

'BEFORE WE START, Mr Czerny-Smith, I need some names and addresses of the friends you visited that night. Just to complete the record.' He liked the sound of this, meaningless but authoritative.

As he expected, Czerny-Smith reacted strongly, beginning to bluster, although not, apparently, out of terror, but from embarrassment. 'I'm afraid I can't tell you any names. Fact is, I wasn't telling the truth. I wasn't visiting friends. I was down on King Street, in a strip bar.'

'Which one?'

'I don't know the name. Just past Sherbourne.'

'All night?'

'More or less. Yes.' He glanced over his shoulder and lowered his voice. 'I picked up someone and went back to her room.'

Salter nearly laughed. It was about as likely as Czerny-Smith claiming he had got into a strip poker game with some strangers. 'All right,' he said. 'Now. I've been looking at the reasons why you might have changed your vote. I looked at your file and at the letters which come after your name in the calendar.' He paused and watched the man grow still. 'How long had Lyall been holding this over your head? Twenty years?'

Czerny-Smith recovered enough to say, 'What?' and make an elaborate gesture of puzzlement, but Salter had his answer. 'Know what?' Czerny-Smith repeated.

'It was blackmail, wasn't it? I thought you might have made a deal—that's what it looked like.'

'A *deal?*' He found some genuine anger. 'A deal! With Lyall? Not in a million years. What kind of deal, may I ask?'

'It looked suspicious. But I know now it was blackmail, wasn't it? If you didn't vote for him he would expose your little dishonesty. He could do it easily when he became dean, or he could use one of the college's popular anonymous notes if he didn't get elected.'

Had Salter been wrong, he would have known by now, but he was right. 'I would have had to resign,' Czerny-Smith said.

'So on Queen Victoria's birthday, you went to tell him what you thought of him. I think you had voted for him under pressure, but it was sticking in your craw, so now you wanted to tell him what you thought of him. There was an argument, a struggle, and he got shot. Don't tell me the details.'

Now that his father was all right, Salter felt like ordering an amnesty for all the prisoners in Metro Toronto, but he just had the disposal of this one. What he planned was to end his involvement in the case by getting a confession from the guilty party and handing the whole thing over to Marinelli. The real villain was dead. He caught a movement in the kitchen which assured him they were being listened to, and continued. 'So, unless you can come up with a better alibi than that, I'm afraid I'm going to have to take you down to headquarters.'

Czerny-Smith gave this some thought. 'You're pretty sure of yourself, aren't you? You are accusing me of murder. All right, then, I can prove where I was that night and I was nowhere near Lyall's.'

'Where were you then?'

'Don't worry, when the time comes I will have a cast-iron alibi, and you will look like a fool. Now ask me why I lied.' Without waiting for the answer, he continued, 'Because you didn't seriously suspect me when you first asked me so I didn't really need an alibi, and I didn't want the truth to get out. I didn't trust you to keep quiet. It doesn't matter now. I'm finished anyway. But now you can wait.'

'Because of the degree thing? Couldn't you just say it was a mistake and change it in the next calendar?'

'It would be all over campus in a week. Why do you think I never applied for chairman? Because I was afraid someone on the committee would notice it in my file. Otherwise the chances were that no one ever would. They wouldn't have either, if. . .'

'What made Lyall check up on you?'

He ignored the question, continuing in his misery. 'It wasn't even my fault. The first president put it in. He was so keen on status that when they printed that first calendar he told them I as good as had it and by the time the calendar was printed I would.'

'Would he confirm that?'

'He's dead. Besides, *he* put it in but *I* left it there.'

'And Lyall blackmailed you.'

'Yes. But I didn't go to his house, and I *certainly* didn't kill him.'

Salter raised his voice slightly and played his last card as loudly as he could. 'I'll get a warrant to search the house, impound your clothes. The evidence will be there.'

'Search away,' Czerny-Smith began, but he was interrupted by his wife coming in from the kitchen.

'Save yourself the trouble. Erroll didn't kill anyone. It was me.'

'The lady in the white coat,' Salter said.

'What?'

'We have an identification.'

'I *was* wearing a white raincoat.'

Czerny-Smith turned in his chair. He thrust out his arm to shut up Salter's questioning, and stood up to face his wife. Salter tried to continue but Czerny-Smith waved him quiet. Finally, his voice twisted into a tortured thread, he said, 'Barbara. You killed him? Because of what he'd done to me?'

'To both of us. Want to hear why?' She turned to Salter. 'You listen, too.'

Salter put away his notebook and sat back.

'When Shirley Marconi switched sides, Erroll came home higher than a kite. Maurice had to lose now. Then he got a call from Maurice and he came home from that little chat and told me that Lyall knew that he didn't have his MA and wanted him to vote for him. Let me finish, dear. Erroll asked me what he should do, and I told him he should vote for Lyall because, you see, *I'd* had a call from Lyall, right after Erroll left him, telling me what he would do which wasn't quite the same thing as he'd said to Erroll.' She was talking to her husband now.

Salter, who thought he knew what was coming,

avoided looking at her or her husband. Czerny-Smith said, 'What is the point of all this?'

'What he told me was that he would tell Erroll how he knew about the degree.'

'That's enough, Barbara.' Czerny-Smith had found a lot of strength from somewhere, enough to take charge of the room. 'He found it in my file, didn't he? Snooping around.'

'He confirmed it from your file, I told you. But I sent him there. I told him. Ten years ago. In bed. And he remembered that and kept it to himself. No one else knew, except me. The night Maurice was killed, Erroll had been stewing about the thing for days, and he'd decided to try to reopen the election and change his vote. Apart from not publicly announcing that he hadn't finished his degree, my husband is a man of high principles, Inspector—'

'It wasn't that. It was the realization that he was going to be my dean, and presumably I'd have to vote his way on every issue for the rest of my time here,' Czerny-Smith interrupted savagely. 'That's how blackmail works.'

Mrs Czerny-Smith continued, standing very close to her husband. 'So he decided he couldn't stand it and was going to tell the world what Lyall had done, bringing everything down but taking Lyall with him. I thought if he tried that, then Lyall might just tell him how he'd found out. But Erroll had been brooding for days by himself, and it came to him what had really happened ten years ago. He confirmed it through...a third party, and came back here and I didn't deny it. I was taking my cue from Erroll, Inspector. Let it all hang out and pick up the pieces later. Erroll, though, took it hard and as of now we are splitting up. Erroll drank a lot of whisky and drove off, and I went to see Lyall.' Her hand was on her husband's shoulder, kneading gently.

'What did you do that for?' Salter asked.

'I'm glad you aren't sure, because I didn't go to kill him. After Erroll left, I had a long think, and realized that I might just be able to give Maurice a taste of his own medicine. What I was going to point out to him was that the next day he was going to be faced with everyone knowing that he had blackmailed Erroll with his secret, which he had got from me in bed. That is, I intended to tell him that if he didn't give up the dean's job quietly, Erroll was in a mood to go to the president and they would both have to resign, Erroll and Maurice, I mean. Me, too, I guess.

'I didn't knock. I just walked in through the back door and up to his room. I found him sitting on the bed with the gun in his hands. He thought I was a robber. We shouted at each other for a long time and . . . the gun went off and I ran away.'

'That's enough,' Czerny-Smith ordered roughly, moving towards her. 'Don't say another word.' He put his hand over her mouth, swinging around to face Salter at the same time. 'Not a word. He hasn't even warned you so you haven't said anything so far.'

'There'll be some evidence on her raincoat,' Salter said. 'No, don't be silly,' holding on to Czerny-Smith as he tried to leave the room. To Mrs Czerny-Smith, he said, 'He's right, though. Don't say another word. Get a lawyer and come down to headquarters tomorrow morning and give yourself up. In the meantime I'll call my office and have your clothes taken to the lab.' He picked up the phone and dialled for help. Czerny-Smith was talking hard, holding on to his wife. 'I don't care about the affair—I'll take early retirement—it was an accident—we'll move...'

Salter said, 'If it hadn't been for your wife's persistence, I might not have cleared Henry Littledeer.' He looked at her. 'Why did you work so hard for him?'

'Don't you see?' Czerny-Smith shouted. 'She couldn't let an innocent man hang.' His new-found strength was ebbing now, turning into hysteria. Now his wife began to hold on to him, supporting him.

'Nobody hangs any more,' Salter said.

Mrs Czerny-Smith said, 'As long as it was only some robber that you hadn't found, I could keep quiet. But, typically, you just picked up some poor Indian who wasn't anywhere near the place. I couldn't let you do that.'

Salter said, 'That the official campus version? From you? The man we arrested had the goods on him from Lyall's house. He was a legitimate suspect.'

'Did he rob the house after I left?'

'It's a complicated story and you'll hear all about it in court. But we didn't grab the first Indian we could find and fill his pockets full of the loot. We questioned a man who was trying to sell Lyall's watch. OK?'

'Sorry. Yes, his lawyer told us that you actually proved his innocence. How did he get the watch?'

'It's a long story, I told you.'

They were interrupted by the arrival of two more policemen. While they were collecting the raincoat and the shoes she had been wearing, Salter remembered that he was supposed to have one more question. 'So where were you that night, Mr Czerny-Smith?'

'Tell him,' his wife urged. She looked across at Salter. 'He's afraid if this gets out it will be bad for his career. But whatever happens to me, we won't be staying, I think. Tell him.'

'I was in prison,' he said, defensive and proud. 'After our argument, I drank some whisky and drove off into the arms of a police cruiser, stopping cars looking for drunken drivers. The RIDE program. I spent the night in the Don Jail.'

Salter affected to look stunned.

'Can I have a question now?' his wife asked. 'You never thought Erroll did it, did you? I could hear from the kitchen. You were just playing games.'

Salter shrugged, saying nothing.

'But how did you know it was me?'

'The boy said from behind you looked just like his mum. Nobody else fitted that description, and the first time I met you it was raining, remember? You were wearing a raincoat. The boy called it white.' He held up a hand. 'And that's enough. Phone a lawyer.'

TWENTY-FOUR

Two DAYS LATER he had one more call to make on the campus, nothing to do with the case.

'I hear,' Wilf Schreiber said, 'that Barbara Czerny-Smith has given herself up. So that was who Lyall dumped. Hell hath no fury, eh, Inspector?'

Salter had no impulse to correct him. Schreiber knew that Judy Kurelek was Lyall's lover; he probably had not worked out the Czerny-Smiths' involvement yet, and was fishing for it now, but Salter could see the possibility of much of the case being dealt with quietly. Let the campus speculate how it liked.

'I'd like to thank you for all your help, Mr Schreiber, and make a suggestion. Don't send any more anonymous notes. None at all. If I hear of one, it will certainly be the last from this office. I thought of charging you with public mischief or something of the sort, and I will if you try it again, but this campus has had enough publicity. I am grateful, though. Without you, we might have sent Henry Littledeer up. But don't write any more.'

He wasn't sure what he wanted. Schreiber simply inflated like a toad and tossed his head. So Salter said it anyway. 'If you are wondering how I found out, it was the oldest, clumsiest, most—what's the word beginning with "b"?—*ordinary* trick in the book. Think back to the chat we had about the notes. Remember saying that there were three? I didn't tell anyone how many; I said "some". I found that trick in a boys' detective story my kid got when he was nine. So don't do it again. We're on to you.'

In many ways it was the best moment of the case. After proving Henry Littledeer innocent, the rest of the events had hardly touched him. Barbara Czerny-Smith would get off lightly, maybe even 'accidental homicide' and failing to report it. Kurelek would be had for disturbing the scene of a crime, but she would be able to plead that she was out of her mind with worry. President Jones had decided, after learning how the degree had been awarded in the calendar by his predecessor, that he would look better if the college stood by Czerny-Smith, whatever happened to his wife. At first he considered leaving the calendar as it was, but it would come out during Barbara's trial, and anyway, Czerny-Smith had insisted on being an honest man, deriving some sort of penitential satisfaction out of reverting to his proper status. When Salter called to tell Professor Usher, to let him know he hadn't buggered up a man's life, Usher had, 'I expect we'll see him every Saturday morning standing outside the St Lawrence Market in his BA gown,' and roared with laughter.

Three weeks later the Crown had decided not to proceed against Judy Kurelek, and had still not set a court appearance for Barbara Czerny-Smith. Shopping in the Eaton Centre, Salter met Joan Dooley who told him she had left the college entirely. 'I wasn't the gal for the job,' she said. 'I'm just not . . . wily enough for the political arena, I guess.'

Salter was inclined to agree, though not so inclined as she was to see her lack of guile as a proof of her natural goodness. Surely one could be wily *and* virtuous? He knew one politician who was. There must be others. 'How's the new dean?' he asked. 'She managing?'

'She? Oh, you mean Jennifer. No, she didn't get it. David Prince did. You remember David, in the Theatre Department? He's a great guy, but Jennifer should have got it.'

'The same committee?'

'All except Erroll. We left him out of it, and agreed not to replace him.'

'Who voted for him?'

'It was unanimous. I was surprised, but Gerald Pentes was for him all along, and Shirley Marconi didn't like Jennifer. And the president told Fred Leitch to vote for David. I didn't have to vote.'

So Schreiber was right. They always win. 'And Schreiber?'

'Wilf assumed that Jennifer would get the job without his help, so he voted for David Prince because that's the way he is.' She looked away. 'I guess from what we heard Maurice kind of brought it on himself.'

No, he didn't, Salter thought. If you lot hadn't told him to dump Judy Kurelek, Shirley Marconi would have voted for him and none of this would have happened. 'Who told the president about Judy Kurelek?' he asked.

She opened her mouth, then backed off. 'Gosh, I don't know now. I'm trying to forget it all.'

Schreiber, Salter thought. He killed Lyall if you unpick it that far back. But this well-meaning, naïve woman had suffered enough. 'You're probably right,' he said. 'He was as much responsible as any one. Will you miss the job?'

'Oh no. I'm in community work now, over in Parkdale with the most terrific bunch of people . . .'

He let her rattle on about her new job without listening until he became aware that she was talking about something else.

'. . . so nobody knows that Maurice was told to stop seeing Judy. They still think he acted on his own. Do you think that's fair? I *worry* about that.'

'Well, don't. What good would it do if they found out? They might think you were the one who told him. Leave it alone. Lotsa luck in the job.' They shook hands and she went on her way.

Early in the summer, Salter visited the Anishnawbe Health Centre to find out if anyone knew what had happened to Henry Littledeer, and received the good news that Henry had gone back up to his reserve, north of Parry Sound. He made a resolution to look him up when he was passing on the way to the fishing cabin he used, but he knew he never would.

The gambling report was nearly finished.

Angus was coming to town, and Salter was looking forward to dandling his grandson on his knee.

And after that, he decided, he needed a sabbatical.

MUDLARK

First Time in Paperback

SHEILA SIMONSON

A LARK DODGE MYSTERY

BEACH BODY

Former book dealer Lark Dodge and her husband, Jay, have traded California for the rustic beaches of Washington State's Shoalwater Peninsula. At first, life is no more complicated than house renovating and baby making. But a carpetbag of dead sea gulls and a corpse on the beach put things on a more adventurous path.

The victim is Cleo Hagen, an outspoken land-development advocate. She's also the ex-wife of Lark's neighbor, a writer whose house mysteriously burns down. And though circumstantial evidence makes him the prime suspect, Lark, with her knack for crime solving, believes there are motives that go much deeper. And what she discovers puts her life in jeopardy.

"An intriguing twist..." —*Publishers Weekly*

Available in June at your favorite retail stores.

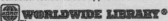

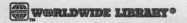

This June , for the first time in paperback

NEW YORK TIMES BESTSELLING AUTHORS:

First
Time in
Paperback

SUE
GRAFTON
TONY
HILLERMAN

and many more...

Bring you

2ND CULPRIT

Newcomers, international names and old favorites offer up a varied itinerary for the adventurous traveler in crime! Join *New York Times* bestselling authors TONY HILLERMAN and SUE GRAFTON, plus an additional cast of 24 of the mystery genre's most popular authors, for 2ND CULPRIT, a choice collection of short stories.

Available in June wherever
Worldwide Mystery books are sold.

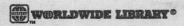

WORLDWIDE LIBRARY ®

2CUL

A
JOHN
COFFIN
MYSTERY

CRACKING OPEN A COFFIN

GWENDOLINE BUTLER

First Time In Paperback

CONFRONTING THE ENEMY

A string of murders that had begun in the past was working its way to the present. The victims were young women whose lives reached from the Second City of London's university to a refuge for battered women—two institutions at opposite ends of the social spectrum, yet connected by death.

Chief Commander John Coffin had seen most varieties of evil in his career, but life had taught him there was always scope for more. The killer in this case seems willing to wait years for the right victim, the right mood. He is fastidious, hard to satisfy, but get them right and he does his job with pleasure.

The complex web of interlocking cases opens a Pandora's box in Coffin's professional and personal life. Too many secrets, too much twisted emotion, too much treachery among friends...one of whom may be a killer.

"An awesome plot.... Truly terrific."   —MLB News

Available in July at your favorite retail stores.

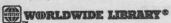

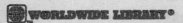